T0346269

## Michael Underwood and The Murder Room

》》 This title is part of The Murder Room, our series dedicated to making available out-of-print or hard-to-find titles by classic crime writers.

Crime fiction has always held up a mirror to society. The Victorians were fascinated by sensational murder and the emerging science of detection; now we are obsessed with the forensic detail of violent death. And no other genre has so captivated and enthralled readers.

Vast troves of classic crime writing have for a long time been unavailable to all but the most dedicated frequenters of second-hand bookshops. The advent of digital publishing means that we are now able to bring you the backlists of a huge range of titles by classic and contemporary crime writers, some of which have been out of print for decades.

From the genteel amateur private eyes of the Golden Age and the femmes fatales of pulp fiction, to the morally ambiguous hard-boiled detectives of mid twentieth-century America and their descendants who walk our twenty-first century streets, The Murder Room has it all. 》》

# The Murder Room
## Where Criminal Minds Meet

themurderroom.com

**Michael Underwood (1916–1992)**

**Michael Underwood** (the pseudonym of John Michael Evelyn) was born in Worthing, Sussex and educated at Christ Church College, Oxford. He was called to the Bar in 1939 and served in the British army during World War Two. He returned to work in the Department of Public Prosecutions until his retirement in 1976, and wrote almost 50 crime novels informed by his career in the law. His five series characters include Sergeant Nick Atwell and lawyer Rosa Epton, of whom is was said by the *Washington Post* that she 'outdoes Perry Mason'.

*By Michael Underwood*

# False Witness

Michael Underwood

An Orion book

Copyright © Isobel Mackenzie 1957

The right of Michael Underwood to be identified as the author of this
work has been asserted in accordance with the Copyright, Designs and
Patents Act 1988.

This edition published by
The Orion Publishing Group Ltd
Orion House
5 Upper St Martin's Lane
London WC2H 9EA

An Hachette UK company
A CIP catalogue record for this book is available from the British Library

ISBN 978 1 4719 0768 5

www.orionbooks.co.uk

To Christianna Brand

# CHAPTER ONE

Jeremy Harper stepped out of the telephone kiosk and stared with a preoccupied frown at the new and gleaming twin-car diesel train that had just deposited him at Seahaven. It looked clean and unromantically efficient as it now waited to make its return journey along the branch line.

Seahaven Station in the middle of the day was an oasis of grimy calm and its depleted staff yawned and sloped about their business with a measured, slothlike purpose.

Suddenly a voice broke in on Jeremy's distant thoughts.

'Train for Franwich Junction platform one, sir', said the owner of a cheerful, freckled face with a porter's cap perched raffishly on the back of his head.

'Eh? . . . er . . . no thanks. I've only just arrived on it', Jeremy said, gathering his thoughts together. He became aware that he was still being grinned at and focusing his gaze, added, 'Oh, hello! I didn't see who it was. How long have you been giving British Railways a hand?'

The grin broadened.

'Started here last week, Mr. Harper. I'm going straight now, you know. Suppose you're here for the Assizes?'

Jeremy nodded and began to return the grin. There had always been something engaging about Sam, he thought, and not only because one of his bouts of uninhibited exuberance had provided Jeremy with his first brief at the Assizes here in his home town. Though admittedly that was something he would remember long after Sam had forgotten the occasion. For the one it had been a landmark, for the other a mere milestone. Jeremy recalled how he had made a passionate plea in mitigation of sentence lasting a full four and a quarter minutes (he had timed it carefully whilst shaving), following which the judge without comment had sent Sam to Borstal.

And now here he was back in Seahaven, cheerful as ever and a fine example of a resilient and forgiving nature.

Jeremy for his part, although only a year or two older than Sam (he was twenty-five to be exact), showed signs on this particular afternoon of having cares disproportionate both to his age and to his professional status as a fledgling barrister. With an abstracted air he listened to Sam's description of a Borstal life whose only drawback, it seemed, had been the lack of female company; and that not as grave as it might have been owing to the strenuous routine of each day and the dog-weariness of Sam each nightfall.

A moment or two later Jeremy was relieved of Sam's presence by a raucous cry of 'tea up' from Seahaven's senior porter, a sinewy old man with a face like a walnut.

Jeremy wandered off through the deserted booking-hall and halted out in the empty station approach. He looked at his watch and then stood staring with furrowed brow across the sun-flecked fields to where the River Fran merged with the sea and the town lay compact on its far bank.

Way off to the right on rising downland lay Sir Geoffrey Rawlins' place, Seahaven Hall. The house itself was hidden from his view by a spinney, but the park was wooded and lushly green. At the opposite end of his line of vision was a group of buildings, surmounted by big black letters which read RAWLINS PAPER MILLS LTD. They represented Sir Geoffrey's first business venture, started thirty years ago when he had been plain and unknown Mr. Rawlins. Now they provided but one of the many sources of a fabulous income. Sir Geoffrey, High Sheriff of the County, ex-Member of Parliament, friend of the great, bonhomous and ruthless. Sir Geoffrey, father of Jennie.

At the thought of Jennie, Jeremy's set look betrayed a fleeting expression of martyrdom. Admittedly he had now grown used to his friends' unspoken commiseration with him about Jennie; but the fact was that for years everyone had assumed that one day they would get married. And that, thought Jeremy for the thousandth time in recent weeks, was the real cause of the trouble. Everyone (including himself) had taken it too much for granted. Everyone, that is, except Jennie. They had not only known each other since childhood but had taken obvious pleasure in each other's company at every stage of their growth from pram to puberty. But while Jeremy's feeling for Jennie slowly turned into love, she never treated him other than as a delightful and useful brother.

Sweet, spoilt Jennie had never begun to realize how secretly hurt he had been by the shattering news of her engagement to Derek Yates. It had been a bombshell whose repercussions were nowhere near ended; though Jeremy had quickly assumed the stiff upper lip that a traditional upbringing had taught him.

Now Jennie was in distress and Jeremy had arrived in Seahaven as a self-appointed avenging angel.

Fixing his eyes sternly on Sir Geoffrey Rawlins' distant paper mill, he took one more look at his watch, picked up his bag and set off down the road.

## CHAPTER TWO

By keeping to the side streets, Jeremy avoided the centre of the town—not that there were very many people about at this hour of an afternoon. The housewives had completed their shopping, the office-workers were back at their desks and a pleasantly somnolent atmosphere prevailed.

He reached the entrance to Queen Elizabeth park and paused to mop his brow. The park which lay at the back of Sir Geoffrey's paper mill was Seahaven's latest source of civic pride; the land having been presented to the town council by a munificent Sir Geoffrey, after he had been forced by circumstances beyond his control to discard less worthy ideas for its use.

Jeremy sniffed tentatively at the sweet lilac-scented air that was wafted towards him and once more looked at his watch.

Suddenly from inside the gate there came a soft rustling sound which caused him to prick his ears and then almost at once everything was silent again. Something kept his senses at the alert, however, and a moment later there was further rustling, this time heavier and more prolonged and terminating in a groan.

Jeremy turned and peered through the park gate in the direction from which the sound had come. As he did so, the groaning restarted. It seemed to come from behind a clump of laurel bushes, and even as Jeremy stared, one of them shook violently and a human arm came groping through the foliage.

'I say, are you in any trouble there?' he called out anxiously, at the same time conscious of the fatuity of his question. For reply there were further and louder groans, mingled with croaks of 'Help!'

Without more ado, Jeremy ran toward the now limp and outflung arm. In the second it took him to do so, his mind began reeling under a succession of imagined headlines—YOUNG BARRISTER IN MURDER DRAMA, SEAHAVEN LAWYER FINDS BODY IN BUSHES, WELL-KNOWN COUNSEL IN PARK DEATH CASE; each more stimulating than the other.

On reaching the laurel bushes, his eye was immediately caught by something shining brightly on the ground. It was a piece of metal chain, loosely dangling at one end; but at the other attached to a wrist. Instinctively he recoiled while a further succession of mind's-eye headlines stormed through his head. This time, however, the well-known Counsel had become the corpse—the victim of a decoy by a dangerous escaped convict.

How long he might have stood there or what he might next have done must remain in the realm of conjecture, since the bushes suddenly parted and a man fell forward at Jeremy's feet.

He was dishevelled; his face was covered with blood and his hair was matted. As Jeremy stared at him in open-mouthed astonishment, he gingerly felt the back of his head. When he took his hand away, it was heavily blood-stained and he groaned again.

'What's happened? Who are you?' Jeremy began uneasily.

'I've been attacked', the injured man gasped and winced with the effort of speaking.

'Attacked? Attacked? But by whom?' The second batch of headlines were not to be lightly dislodged and there was something ominous about the chain that hung from the man's wrist. 'And that ...' Jeremy added, nodding at it.

'This, you mean?' the man asked, waving the chain in Jeremy's direction and looking at it ruefully. 'I had the firm's wages in a bag on the end of that.'

'Good Lord', Jeremy said incredulously. 'But ... but ... then it's not a handcuff?'

'Handcuff? ... Oh, I suppose it does look a bit like one.' He stared in a dazed manner at the length of broken chain. 'The men who coshed me had a pair of wire-cutters with them.'

'Do you mean you've been robbed?'

'Of eight thousand pounds.'

There was a moment's silence and then, pulling himself together, Jeremy said, 'I'll go and phone the police. And what about an ambulance, or do you think you can walk?'

The man got shakily to his feet, clutching at Jeremy for support. While he did so, Jeremy studied him closely. He looked about thirty and was tall and good-looking in a rather film-starish way, having a small black moustache and white even teeth.

'Thanks', he said, panting. 'I think I can manage, with your help. Yes, we must get through to the police and I must also phone my firm.' The thought of this brought his stumbling footsteps to a halt and he added in a despairing tone, 'They must have got miles away by now. The couple who robbed me, I mean. God, what a mess...'

'Look, you sit on this seat while I go and phone the police and report what's happened.'

'Could you also get a message through to my firm? It's Rawlins Paper Mills, the place over there the other side of the park. Tell them I've been attacked and robbed of all the wages.' He paused and added more to himself than to Jeremy, 'By now they'll have guessed something's up.' He closed his eyes in apparent pain. 'I'm sorry, but it's my head. It feels as though it's got a steam hammer inside it.'

'That's all right, you rest here. I won't be gone long.' Jeremy was about to depart but suddenly turned back. 'By the way, I'd better know your name.'

'Me? I'm the cashier at the mill', said the man. 'My name's Yates. Derek Yates.'

# CHAPTER THREE

Detective-Sergeant Raymond Floyd, head of the Seahaven C.I.D., was doing his football pools when news of the crime reached him. He gave a low, interested whistle as he replaced the telephone receiver and quickly shoved the pools form out of sight.

The Criminal Investigation Department was installed on the first floor of an old house which was wholly unsuitable for the purpose. Bare boards, now dangerously rutted by the constant passage of feet, set the tone of dingy discomfort that prevailed. Round the walls, flimsy plywood cupboards burst with dog-eared files, and trestle tables were covered with the same bizarre assortment of articles as is seen in most C.I.D. offices. Loose papers, blood-stained blunt instruments, stolen valuables and strange pieces of wearing apparel were all lumped together, waiting to play their part in sending someone to prison. Even the bathroom had been pressed into use and converted into a photographic dark-room.

Sergeant Floyd's own office had once been a dressing-room: a poky one at that. But for several reasons he preferred to have a small room to himself than to share a larger one with subordinate members of his staff, who at the time comprised three detective-constables, a uniformed officer on attachment and two girl clerks.

As for Floyd himself, he was an efficient and industrious officer; though his natural inability to ingratiate himself with his superiors had resulted in his being passed over for promotion and in a consequently sour outlook on life. Got a bit of a chip on his shoulder, his fellow officers in the force were wont to say with varying degrees of charity. Perhaps the most remarkable thing about him was that no one had ever seen him dressed otherwise than from head to foot in brown.

Accompanied by Detective-Constable Ingram, he now left immediately for the scene of the crime and arrived to find Derek Yates sprawled on one of the park seats, his head thrown back and a handkerchief pressed against his bleeding cheek. At the opposite end of the seat, Jeremy hovered uncertainly, as though reluctant to be thought associated with the injured man.

With an air of weary forbearance, Yates answered Sergeant Floyd's preliminary questions which elicited the bare outline of what had happened.

'O.K., Mr. Yates', Floyd said briskly, when he had gleaned the minimum necessary to launch his inquiries. 'Detective-Constable Ingram will take you along to the hospital to get you patched up and then if you're not detained I'll want you to come back to the police station and give a full statement. In the meantime, I'll have a look around here to see if your attackers have left any clues.' As he finished speaking, he fixed Jeremy with a dispassionate eye and added, 'You can wait and come back with me. O.K.?'

'Well, actually I was on my way home. My mother will be expecting me.'

'That's easily arranged. Ingram'll phone her and say you'll be a bit late. O.K.?'

'I suppose so, but I can't see...'

'Right; let's not waste any more time', Floyd broke in before Jeremy could complete the sentence. He turned to Detective-Constable Ingram who was standing beside a hesitant Yates. 'Go on, away with you', he said peremptorily.

Jeremy said nothing. Silently he had decided, however, that the time would undoubtedly come when he would remind Sergeant Floyd that an amiable manner should not be mistaken for weakness. They knew one another, of course, through Jeremy being a barrister with local connections, and Sergeant Floyd had never taken any pains to hide his contempt for all the struggling young Counsel with whom he came into official contact. He regarded them as a regimental sergeant-major might a bunch of newly-commissioned subalterns, and Jeremy

11

was aware of it.

As they walked to the point where Yates had indicated he'd been attacked, Floyd shot him a sidelong glance and said:

'Wonder if this'll make Sir Geoffrey like his future son-in-law any better?'

'I've no idea', Jeremy replied coldly.

'You knew who he was, of course, didn't you?' Floyd went on. 'Yates, I mean.'

'Not until he told me his name.'

'Not before?'

'No, why should I have?'

'Just thought you would have, that's all.' He stopped in the vicinity of a purple lilac tree and peered closely about him. Jeremy halted at his side and Floyd said, 'Can you see anything here connected with a recent robbery?'

'I don't think so.'

'Nor can I. Let's see: it's about forty to fifty yards from here to where you found him. Forty or fifty yards of trees and bushes. Nice secluded spot. Anything strike you as significant about it?'

Jeremy shook his head, determined not to thaw.

'I'm surprised at that and you a budding young barrister, with a ritzy education. Ah well! perhaps it's lucky for us dumb police that you're not all as clever as foxes.' Jeremy's stony expression seemed to amuse him, but changing his tone, he continued, 'Since you're likely to be a witness and not an advocate in this case—that is if it ever gets as far as a prosecution—I'll tell you what strikes me as odd. It's this. What was a cashier doing with his firm's wages in the loneliest part of a deserted park on a quiet afternoon?' The question was accompanied by a piercing stare.

'I suppose he ...' Jeremy began and let the sentence trail away when no reasonable explanation came to him.

After a second's silence, Sergeant Floyd shrugged his shoulders impatiently.

'Don't bother to suppose anything, Mr. Harper. We'll get back to the Station and ask him.' He took a final look around. 'There certainly doesn't seem to be anything here to help us. No torn-off buttons, no handy fibres caught on bushes, no tell-tale footprints, no nothing.' He chewed at his lower lip and said thoughtfully, 'They materialize from nowhere, they rob and they melt away again without trace.'

'Good heavens, yes. You don't think ... I mean all those recent robberies that have been reported in the papers.'

Floyd nodded.

'All very much of a pattern and all bearing the trademark of the same outfit. In every instance a cashier gets waylaid and relieved of the wages bag.' He paused and went on, 'How much did Yates say he had with him?'

'Eight thousand pounds.'

'Eight thousand pounds, eh? Someone's getting infernally rich. And paying no taxes on it either.'

\*     \*     \*

Sergeant Floyd and Jeremy arrived at the C.I.D. office at almost the same moment as Yates and Detective-Constable Ingram. Yates's head was swathed in white bandages, over the top of which a lock of black hair peeped. He looked pale and walked stiffly from the car to the door of the building.

After a quick word with Ingram, Sergeant Floyd turned to him and said:

'I gather you've suffered no serious damage, Mr. Yates. Injuries often look worse than they are, thanks to lots of blood.'

'All I know is I've got the hell of a headache', Yates said wanly.

'An aspirin or two will soon put that right. Come up to the office and we'll get that statement on paper. You too', he added, nodding in Jeremy's direction.

On their arrival in the main office, a space was cleared at one of the cluttered tables and Ingram arranged chairs for the two visitors.

'Now let's hear the story from the beginning and then we'll decide what to put down.'

Derek Yates ran the tip of his tongue over his

lips and leant forward, resting his clasped hands on the edge of the table. He was about to speak when Sergeant Floyd broke in.

'Wait a moment, let's get this question out of the way first. What were you doing in the park with the firm's wages? You normally go to and from the bank in one of their cars, don't you?'

'Yes, and that's what I want to explain', Yates said. 'You know there've been a lot of these robberies recently? Well, last week on the way to the bank, I was almost certain our car was trailed—I mentioned it to the driver—there was nothing particularly sinister about this other vehicle except that it kept a steady distance behind us all the way. It never attempted to overtake but just stuck on our tail.'

'Same thing happen on the way back?'

'No, it didn't and that's why I never reported the matter. I thought I must have imagined it after all.' Nobody said anything and Yates went on, 'This afternoon I was again quite certain we were followed—though it was a different car from last week—and so I told the driver to go back alone, and that after drawing the money I'd slip out of a side door of the bank and return on foot avoiding our usual route.' He paused ruefully. 'I can only imagine that they spotted me and decided to waylay me in the park. It's a pretty humiliating thought that I must have made it easier for them.'

'You were certainly a good deal more vulnerable there than you would have been in the car', Sergeant Floyd agreed. Yates nodded tensely and Floyd went on, 'And what exactly happened in the park? Remember, every detail may be important.'

'My idea was to walk round the top of the park by all those bushes and enter the mill the back way. I'd got to the spot I showed you, when suddenly I heard a sound just behind me and to the right. As I turned, I received a blow on top of the head and then ... well, then everything seemed to happen at once. I was hit over the head again and someone seized the cash bag from my hand and cut the chain by which it was fastened to my wrist. By that time I was fairly groggy and more or less down on my knees and the men ran off. After that ...'

'In which direction did they go?'

'Towards the gate.'

'Along the path?'

'How do you mean?'

'Did they run off along the path or dive back into the cover of the bushes?'

For a moment Yates hesitated as three pairs of eyes watched him intently.

'They disappeared into the bushes again.'

'Right. Now give me a description of the men. There were two of them, I gather?'

'Yes, that's all I saw. One was of medium height and the other was short and stocky. It was the taller one who struck me while the other seized the money.'

'What about their faces? Complexions? Colour of hair? Shapes of their noses? I want everything you can remember about them.'

'The trouble is I can remember very little. It all happened so suddenly and the next thing I knew I was lying dazed on the ground.'

'Tell me the little you can remember', Floyd urged.

'I know they both had hats pulled well down over their faces. I never really saw their features at all.'

'You must have noticed something more about them.'

Yates shook his head.

'I could easily let my imagination go and give you a detailed portrait of each of them. But quite frankly they wouldn't be of the men who were there: just what I've since persuaded myself they looked like.'

'Let's hear that anyway. We may find the descriptions tally with some of our old clients.'

'I'm sorry, Sergeant, but I keep on trying to explain I can't describe them at all.'

There ensued a silence in which Floyd fished energetically inside his left ear with his little finger and stared at Yates with an air of surly appraisal.

Jeremy for his part had sat back in his chair during the interrogation. His face was pale, his expression tense and his eyes had never for one moment wavered from Yates.

Though he had already assumed those of the Bar's mannerisms necessary to impress clients with his sagacity and *savoir-faire*, he looked, with brown curly hair and a boyish figure, younger than his years. In almost every aspect of character he was the antithesis of Yates, who, from all accounts, affected to find and take his pleasures easily and was possessed of abundant surface charm, at any rate where women were concerned. In addition, Yates had the further inestimable advantage for an Englishman of being good at sport. Ambition too he certainly had and it was this allied to his other talents that had encouraged him to propose marriage to Jennie Rawlins, who was his eminent boss's daughter and a prize seemingly miles beyond his social reach.

These were the matters that occupied Jeremy's thoughts as he sat silently watching and listening.

'We'll get some of this down on paper', Floyd said at length, disengaging his little finger.

It all took quite a long time and afterwards there was Jeremy's own statement to be recorded, so that it was after six o'clock before he and Yates were able to leave.

As they got up, Floyd turned to Yates and with a laugh that carried no humour, said:

'I wouldn't worry too much about the money.

Sir Geoffrey'll simply knock it off your wedding present.'

Ignoring this tasteless pleasantry and biting nervously at his thumbnail, Yates asked:

'I suppose there's not much hope of recovering the money?'

'You never know. Everyone slips up sooner or later. *Everyone.*'

Yates shot him a quick glance.

'But you've no idea who's behind these robberies?' The inflection by which the sentence was turned into a question was so slight that Sergeant Floyd could have properly pretended not to have noticed it.

'You leave us to get on with the job', he said. 'You can rest assured that when we want the assistance of either you or Mr. Harper again, we shan't be slow in asking for it.'

★     ★     ★

Jeremy and Derek Yates left the building together, but once outside went their separate ways without speaking. Indeed they hadn't exchanged a word since leaving the park. On finally parting company, Yates appeared so heavily preoccupied as to be oblivious of Jeremy's presence and Jeremy himself was not without some pressing thoughts.

As soon as he had had supper and with commendably concealed exasperation had assuaged an onset of maternal curiosity in his recent activities (Mrs. Harper was a widow and Jeremy her only son), he excused himself, borrowed his mother's car and drove up to the Hall to see Jennie who, he knew, was waiting for him with gnawing impatience.

On rounding the last bend of the drive, he saw Sir Geoffrey's new dove-grey Rolls-Bentley parked before the front door. The angle at which it stood and the heavy score marks made in the gravel by its wheels clearly indicated to someone who knew how to interpret the signs that Sir Geoffrey had arrived home in not the most equable of moods.

Before Jeremy was able to get out of his car Jennie, who had been on the terrace listening for him, came hurrying round the side of the house.

'I thought you were never coming', she said as she rushed forward to greet him.

Jeremy gave her an indulgent smile and allowed himself to be borne away to the terrace where coffee and a tray of drinks were set out.

'Here's your coffee,' Jennie said, thrusting a cup at him. 'You did want black, didn't you?' she added as an afterthought. 'And have a liqueur?' She picked up a bottle of Crème de Menthe and squinted at it. 'I suppose you don't like the pretty ones. I know; what about this? Kümmel: colourless and quite revolting.' But Jeremy asked for brandy and Jennie murmured vaguely, 'I think there's some in one of these bottles.'

A moment later, armed with his coffee and brandy, he walked over to the swing seat and waited for Jennie to join him. As he watched her pouring herself a drink, he experienced such a sharp pang that he quickly turned away lest she should notice his expression. Jennie with her mop of fair curly hair, her deliciously healthy complexion and her short, just right figure had set many a male breast hopefully pounding in the last few years. It was true to say, however, that only two men had ever really captured her notice. Jeremy, dear faithful Jeremy; and Derek. The one she liked more than anyone she knew; but it was the other she loved and who made her melt and tingle every time she saw him, and who filled her with such longing that her every joint began to ache.

If it had been one of the so-called eligible young men she met by the dozen (many of them with good looks, several with as much money as Jennie herself was one day likely to inherit, a few with noble family ties and one even who qualified under each of these heads) Jeremy would have faded gracefully from the scene with no more than a wistful backward glance. But it wasn't one of these. It was Derek Yates with his smooth looks and acquired social graces to whom Jennie was surrendering herself with such single-minded purpose, and for weeks past Jeremy had been subject to violent alternations of feeling in the matter. One moment he was accepting it with fatalism and the unquestioning loyalty of a high civil servant out of sympathy with his government's policy. The next, however, his mind was poring over practical measures for queering Yates's pitch.

It was, he recalled, in the former mood that he had arrived in Seahaven that afternoon—but much had happened since then.

Jennie came across to where he was standing and together they sat down.

'When did you hear about it?' he asked.

'They phoned up from the mill about four o'clock and I took the message. Daddy was out but he called in there on his way back from London.'

'Where's your father now?'

'In his study.'

'Has he said anything about it?'

Jennie gave a short, bitter laugh.

'He didn't need to. His manner when he got home was sufficient comment in itself. There's something I must ask you, Jeremy', she went on, turning her head and fixing him with a searching look. Her eyes which were large and a deep blue met his and held them. Jeremy swallowed uncomfortably. 'Was it really a coincidence that you happened to be in the park when Derek was robbed?'

'But I wasn't', he expostulated. 'I only

arrived there when it was all over.'

'You were still the first person on the scene. Was that coincidence?'

'Well, of course it was', he said with what was meant to sound like a reassuring laugh. 'Whatever's going through your head? Why, I'd never met Yates before. I didn't even know who he was until he told me his name.'

'I know', Jennie said thoughtfully. 'That's what makes it such a coincidence.'

'Look, Jennie, I don't know what you're getting at, but I wish you'd stop hinting mysterious things.'

'I'm sorry, Jeremy dear', she said contritely. 'The truth is everything's in such a hopeless mess, I don't really know what I'm thinking.'

Jeremy put out a hand and lightly caressed one of hers.

'You've been having a rough time these past few weeks', he said gently.

She kicked defiantly at a pebble.

'Daddy has forbidden me to see Derek until this matter's cleared up.'

'Forbidden?'

'As good as. He didn't actually use that word because he knew it would be the surest way of speeding me to Derek's side. But he's said it would be best if I didn't see him for a day or so, as it might embarrass him and the police ... and practically everyone else in Seahaven it seems.'

'Has . . .' Jeremy began and then hesitated. 'Has . . . Derek been in touch with you this evening?'

Jennie shook her head and then as though to explain the omission, said:

'There's no phone at his lodgings.'

'When did you last see him?'

'Oh, a few days ago', she replied in a casual tone that deceived neither of them. Gazing out across the soft green park to the distant woods, she went on, 'It's so incredibly unfair the way everyone has treated him since we became engaged. He's been made to feel he was a plain, money-grubbing adventurer. Oh, people have been polite in a double-edged sort of way, but I know the kind of things they've been saying behind our backs. I wish now we'd run away and got married without a word to anyone. We very nearly did, you know.' She paused and added in a bitter tone, 'It's no wonder Derek's become a bit disillusioned.'

'Disillusioned?' Jeremy said with surprise.

'Yes, about marrying into the so-called upper classes', Jennie replied fiercely.

Jeremy wondered whether that was the true cause of the disillusionment and indeed whether disillusionment properly described Yates's present outlook. He refrained, however, from asking what else he, Yates, had expected following a first meeting with his boss's daughter at a staff dance and a bitterly opposed announcement of their engagement less than two months later. That Sir Geoffrey *had* eventually consented to the engagement was taken by no one, who knew him, to be a final capitulation. In fact he had made it very plain to Yates that this was to be no short cut to an easy life and that talent, if he possessed any, would be more than ever required to establish his claim to a brighter future.

When expediency required Sir Geoffrey to make a withdrawal, it was not only a fighting one but counter-attacks could also be very much expected.

Jeremy was about to reply to Jennie's defence of her fiancé's behaviour when he heard footsteps behind him. He looked round to see Sir Geoffrey and sprang to his feet.

'Good evening, sir', he said in his most cordial tone.

'Hello, Jeremy. Wait a moment, I think I'll get myself a drink.' Sir Geoffrey turned back to the tray of bottles on the table by the french window. He was still in his town clothes; a dark grey suit, cream silk shirt and dark red polka-dot bow tie. His monocle on the end of a broad black ribbon hung loosely over his navel and not a hair in his rich silver mane was out of place. A sensual mouth was set in a face whose expression could change with alarming suddenness from carefree affability to cold and frightening anger. There was never any doubt that he enjoyed playing the great man and, if he didn't always measure up to the genuine article, he was nevertheless a remarkable person.

He came over to the swing seat, drink in hand and pulling a chair behind him. He sat down, took a deep draught and noisily sucking his lips, said:

'I've had a damned tiring day, Jeremy. Nothing but meetings. A Board one in the City this morning and a long, exhausting one at the Treasury this afternoon. And when I finally get home, looking forward to a nice peaceful week-end, I'm greeted with the news that eight thousand pounds of the mill's wages have been spirited away.' Jeremy assumed an interested expression, but could think of no suitable comment. 'But of course you know all about that. Good of you to help the way you did', Sir Geoffrey added with a patronizing air.

'I imagine you're insured against such contingencies, aren't you, sir?' Jeremy said, feeling that something more than facial contortion should be attempted.

Sir Geoffrey looked at him sharply.

'I've no doubt that's one of many things they'll be looking into.' The 'they' referred to the host of able lieutenants who were paid to concern themselves with the day-to-day running of his various enterprises.

'It's about time the police got on to the master-mind behind all these robberies',

Jeremy said. 'He'll probably turn out to be a pillar of civic respectability.' Unaware of Sir Geoffrey's changing expression, he continued, 'This must be the fourth major one in as many weeks. A haul of over twenty thousand quid isn't bad going, especially when, as Sergeant Floyd was saying, it's tax free.'

'That's your theory, is it? That this was an organized gang job?' Sir Geoffrey asked in a tone that was ominously quiet.

'It seems the obvious one, don't you think, sir? I gather it's what the police are working on too.'

Sir Geoffrey pursed his lips.

'We shall doubtless see', he murmured. Then stretching his arms he said genially with another sudden change of mood, 'What a glorious evening and the countryside's looking wonderful. Did you notice the Judas tree as you came up the drive? You can just see it from the second bend. It's a mass of purple blossom. I've never seen it lovelier. Pity is I can't transplant it somewhere I could see it from the house. It's wasted down there.' He gave his daughter a twinkling look. 'But what's the use of having a garden full of lovely things when you have a daughter who takes no interest in it?'

Speaking for the first time since her father had come out on to the terrace, Jennie said:

'I like the garden very much. In fact I love it. It's only gardening I dislike.' She gave her father the shadow of a smile. 'Be the truth known, I probably know more about botany than you do, Daddy.'

'Hmm, pity you . . .' Sir Geoffrey began but stopped. He had been on the verge of making an acid reference to an early incident in his daughter's courtship by Derek Yates—in fact it had been the first occasion he had met his prospective son-in-law socially and Yates's single lapse throughout a difficult evening had been to gaze admiringly at a still-life painting of Sir Geoffrey's prize polyanthus and declare that primroses were one of his favourite flowers—when a warning look from Jennie cut the sentence short.

After some further desultory conversation, Jennie got up and pulled her cardigan tightly round her shoulders.

'It's getting chilly. I'm going in.' She turned to Jeremy. 'Would you mind dropping something for Sylvia at the lodge on your way home?' Without waiting for a reply, she disappeared through the french window and returned a moment later with a paper-back crime book. 'It's got Sylvia's name in it, so presumably it's hers. I found it amongst some old papers on the hall table.'

Jeremy accepted his cue (somewhat reluctantly since there were still a number of things he wished to say to Jennie but for her father's presence) and a few moments later was free-wheeling down the drive.

★    ★    ★

Sylvia Ainsworth was the daughter of Jennie's old nurse and lived in the lodge at the main entrance to the Hall. The old nurse had been pensioned off there and had since died, but Sylvia stayed on by the grace of Sir Geoffrey. She was often away, however, having a job in the Clerk of the Assize's office.

Seahaven was the first Assize town of six on the Coastal Circuit, with the result that apart from vacations and the three times a year when the Assizes were held at Seahaven itself, she spent her time living out of a suitcase. With the Clerk of Assize, Clerk of Indictments and two others (one of each sex) she formed the staff that administered the Circuit and moved from Assize town to Assize town like a travelling circus, lugging with them huge hampers which contained all the impedimenta necessary to itinerant justice.

Over several years she had earned the reputation of being the indispensable member of the troupe; the one to whom the others were frequently beholden and whom solicitors and barristers' clerk most often approached with their perennial tangles.

As Jeremy got out of the car and pushed through the smart little swing gate that gave

entry to Sylvia's trim domain, he heard the
sound of voices inside the lodge. For no good
reason this surprised him. In so far as he had
given any thought to the matter at all, he'd
somehow always imagined that once away from
Court Sylvia retired into a sort of vacuumatic
shell, and the idea that she might have friends
and entertain them had never occurred to him.

He tapped lightly on the front door and stood
back a pace. The voices ceased and a second
later framed in the open doorway was Hubert
Waygood. The Clerk of Indictments looked his
usual, perky self and quite unabashed by
Jeremy's presence on the doorstep.

'Hello, Mr. Harper', he said chirpily. 'What
can we do for you? You haven't tracked me
down to try and do a fiddle over that case of
yours that's coming up on Monday, I hope.'

Small, sandy-haired and inordinately pleased
with himself, Hubert Waygood always chose to
believe that everyone connected with the
Coastal Circuit spent their time importuning
him for favours. It was an infuriating and
incurable habit. Many attempts had been made
to break him of it but a combination of vanity
and monumental self-confidence had armour-
plated him against everything from subtle
mockery to blunt sarcasm. Though Mr.
Swinbank, the Clerk of Assize, was the only
member of the small staff who was a qualified
lawyer, the Clerk of Indictments strove

ceaselessly to give the impression that he too belonged professionally.

'As a matter of fact, you may be surprised to learn I haven't called here to see *you* at all', Jeremy was stung to reply.

'No, I guessed that from the look on your face when I opened the door', Waygood said with a maddening grin.

'Is Miss Ainsworth in?' Jeremy asked, trying to peer past him into the hall.

'She is, but she's not very well at the moment. A bit worked up, you know, but I'm making her a cup of tea and she'll be O.K.' He noticed Jeremy's expression and continued, 'You know what women are. Sometimes they get upset over nothing.'

Jeremy had no idea what Waygood was trying to say and even less wish to get involved in his personal affairs. It seemed, however, that there might be something, after all, in the local rumours which had Waygood, some twenty years older than Sylvia, proposing marriage to her at least once every Assize. He was about to hand the book to Waygood when Sylvia herself suddenly appeared in the hall.

'Good evening, Mr. Harper', she said. 'I thought I recognized your voice.'

'I was just explaining to him that you're not feeling too good', Waygood said officiously.

Sylvia threw him an exasperated look and said:

'There's nothing wrong with me at all. At least nothing that being left alone won't put right.'

'There you are; I told you she wasn't herself this evening', Waygood said, jerking his head in her direction.

'Miss Jennie asked me to give you this book as I passed', Jeremy said quickly, holding it out. 'She found it at the Hall and I gather it's yours.'

Sylvia took the book and turned it over carefully as if it were some rare species. Then in a faintly puzzled tone she said:

'Oh, I see. Thank you.'

'I think I hear the kettle boiling', Waygood said and started to go back in when Sylvia put out a hand.

'Do you mind, but I'd like you to leave now. I'm sure Mr. Harper'll give you a lift into Seahaven.'

'I'll just make your tea first.'

'No', Sylvia said firmly. 'Please go.'

For some moments Waygood studied her face with darting eyes.

'I don't mind stopping if you want me to', he said.

'But I *don't* want you to.'

'Well, if there's nothing else I can do, I'll be getting along', he said, shrugging his shoulders. 'See you in the morning, Sylvia. Don't be late; we've got to check those exhibits in the

Myerson case. G'night.'

The front door shut before the two men could turn away from the porch.

Jeremy was determined not to be drawn into further discussion of the episode, though he couldn't help pondering over it. Sylvia had certainly not been her usual calm, unruffled self. Her face had been flushed and she had seemed on edge.

He need not have worried, however, for Hubert Waygood was far too much of an extrovert to waste time speculating on the whys and wherefores of female behaviour. On the drive back into town he treated Jeremy to a tediously detailed account of his prowess on the croquet lawn. He was an enthusiastic player and a crashing bore on the subject. By the time he deposited him in the main square, Jeremy was heartily wishing there was a handy croquet mallet in the car.

# CHAPTER FOUR

The next day was Saturday (a gloriously sunny one as befitted the month of May) and by early afternoon most of Seahaven's denizens had gone off to disport themselves smiting and chasing balls of various colours and sizes.

Amongst these was Hubert Waygood who,

decked out in flannels, blue blazer and white panama hat, was the cynosure of all eyes on the municipal croquet lawn. Supremely contented, but confident that this was no more than his due, he had no thought for anything other than his afternoon's sport—certainly none for the future, which was probably quite a good thing and in large measure responsible for his happy spirit.

Jeremy unfortunately was only able to enjoy such of the sun as shone obliquely through his bedroom window. Immediately after lunch he had retired there to master the ramifications of his brief for the defence in a case due for trial at the Assizes on Monday. He was representing a scoundrel who had defrauded a string of housewives by obtaining their orders (and money) for yet another new, miraculous (but in this case non-existent) detergent. He appeared to have no defence to the charges and to add public insult to private injury was now being defended, via Jeremy, at public expense. This meant that, though the case might enrich Jeremy's experience, it certainly wouldn't do the same for his pocket. For the tenth time in as many minutes, he laboriously dragged his mind back to the schedule of figures on the desk before him.

Detective-Sergeant Floyd was another who was spending the afternoon at work. He had been at Rawlins Paper Mill most of the morning, nosing around and asking a lot of questions. Now he was doggedly correlating the results of his inquiries so far. Detective Chief Inspector Adams from County police headquarters at Franwich was due to call in and Floyd looked forward to presenting him with some interesting suggestions regarding the robbery.

Up at Seahaven Hall, Sir Geoffrey, after a morning also spent at the mill, had retired for a siesta and Jennie, frustrated and bored, had taken the dogs for a walk. Earlier she had tried to make surreptitious contact with Derek Yates but without success.

As she wandered along one of the grassy tracks which ran through the woods, her mind flitted incontinently over recent events and it was some time before she realized that Sambo, the black Labrador, had disappeared. She whistled and called his name without response. Putting him out of her mind, she wandered a further fifty yards or so and then stopped once more. This time when she called, he came bursting out of the cover of some rhododendron bushes close to her father's beloved Judas tree. He gave his mistress a quick, approving look before gambolling off ahead of her down the track. By this time Sadie, the Sealyham, had vanished and Jennie spent further fruitless seconds trying to attract the dog's attention. With a hopeless sigh she started off again just as there came the sound of Sambo's furious but delighted barks round the next bend. She hurried forward and there suddenly was Derek with Sambo jumping around him with quite unwonted enthusiasm.

'Darling!' Jennie cried as she rushed into his arms. 'Sambo, get down. Darling, I do believe he's as excited at seeing you as I am. Oh, how wonderful and I was having such a horrid afternoon.' She gazed adoringly into Derek's face. 'Are you quite all right?' she asked anxiously, putting a gentle hand up to the piece of sticking plaster above his right eye which was the only remaining sign of his encounter in the park. She ran her hand down his cheek and started to tremble. 'Kiss me, Derek', she whispered.

He bent down his head and did so. Jennie clung passionately to his lips. When he broke free of her, he said with a small tolerant smile:

'What with you *and* Sambo, I'll soon be groggier than I was yesterday after I'd been clonked over the head.'

Taking a neatly folded handkerchief out of his pocket, he carefully wiped his mouth and moustache. Jennie watched him with a worried expression.

'Thank goodness I happened to meet you, darling. Think how awful it would have been if you'd got up to the Hall and found I was out.'

Derek Yates said nothing and just smiled

down at her. It was a curious smile, though Jennie was far too happy to notice anything particular about it.

'Let's go and sit over on that tree and talk', she went on, indicating the trunk of a felled sycamore. 'I want to hear all about what happened yesterday.' She paused and with a small pout added, 'Daddy's told me I shouldn't see you till the whole matter's cleared up, which is ridiculous, isn't it?'

Derek Yates was not, however, very forthcoming about his recent experience and when she chided him, he said:

'I'm sorry but I'm fed up with talking about it. I had to spend most of the morning answering a lot of silly questions by Sergeant Floyd and I'd like to think about something else for a change.'

'I understand, darling. Let's just hope it all gets cleared up quickly so that we can go ahead with our wedding plans.' She nestled close to his side and laid her cheek against his shoulder. With a vaguely abstracted air, he kissed her quickly on the mouth and then turned his head away to stare moodily at the two dogs who were digging furiously in an old rabbit burrow a few yards away.

'Was there something particular you were coming to see me about?' Jennie asked in a hopeful tone, breaking the silence that had overtaken them.

He shook his head.

'Just to see you, Jennie', he said with a tender smile and kissed her on the forehead.

'What were you going to do if you saw Daddy?'

'Say good afternoon and inquire after his primroses.' They both laughed.

'Did he speak to you at the mill this morning?'

'No, I never even saw him, though word gets round quickly enough when he's on the premises.'

Another silence fell, broken by Jennie who said:

'When are we going to get married, darling? I can't bear to wait much longer.' With a trace of desperation in her tone she went on, 'Why can't we go off and settle down miles away from Seahaven: miles away from anyone who knows us. Why can't we, Derek?'

'But your father and your position . . . ?'

'What do they matter? I don't care if Daddy *does* cut me out of his will, and *you* could earn far more money than you get at the mill. Darling, do let's; otherwise I'm sure we'll never get married. There are so many influences at work against us here.'

'I know how you feel, Jennie', he said. 'But we've had all this out before and I thought'—here his voice became gently reproachful—'that we'd agreed it was best to win over your father and the rest of the world slowly rather than antagonize everyone by hasty action. Gretna Green's all right for newspaper headlines but...'

'I know, I know', Jennie broke in impatiently. 'Trouble is I'm too impetuous and you're too practical.'

'And it's a darned shame we can't make a compromise', he said soothingly and, before Jennie could voice any further anxieties, took her head in both his hands and kissed her long and generously.

It was the sound of a twig snapping that finally brought them apart. There, standing a few yards distant and very deliberately not looking in their direction, was Sylvia.

Jennie got up and smoothed the front of her dress.

'Hello, Sylvia, we ... we didn't see you coming', she said awkwardly and went on quickly, 'I don't think you know my fiancé.' She turned towards Derek Yates. 'Derek, this is Miss Ainsworth. It's she who lives in the lodge. You may have seen her as you've gone in and out.'

Derek and Sylvia exchanged small nods accompanied by appropriate murmurs and there followed a silence in which Sylvia, looking coolly attractive, stood with her fists balled in the pockets of her cardigan, and gazed at Jennie and Derek with an air of detachment. Jennie linked a proprietorial arm through Derek's and said:

'I expect you've heard what a horrible experience he had yesterday.'

'Yes, it's in all the papers', Sylvia replied in a brief, matter-of-fact tone.

Jennie immediately felt herself bridling. So Sylvia thought she too could join in the cold war against Derek, did she? Sylvia who but for Rawlins' charity would be paying to live in some drab room. This Sylvia who now couldn't even make a pretence at conventional politeness; offer a word of sympathy; or show a flicker of interest. Jennie looked at her with hostility but Sylvia's own thoughts seemed to be elsewhere as she stood watching the dogs hard at their burrowing. She's so gauche, she won't even *leave* us now, Jennie thought furiously. She looked at Derek who had been standing like a pillar of salt for the past few minutes. His forehead was furrowed and he almost looked to be in a state of suspended animation. Each one of the three appeared to be waiting for something to happen without knowing what. Finally it was Sylvia who broke the silence.

'I think I'll be getting along', she said. 'I was just having a short stroll before tea. Good-bye.' She gave Derek a small nod and turning on her heel walked off along the track.

'Most probably she's sex-starved', Jennie snorted at her departing back. 'I mean, there must be some explanation for her behaviour. She's always been *fairly* reserved, but today she was plain rude.'

'I didn't think she was', Yates replied.

'I did. Fancy her not saying a word to you about yesterday.'

'Perhaps the subject embarrassed her. After all, she works in the Assize office, didn't you say? And when the case comes for trial, I suppose I'm bound to be the chief witness.'

'I don't know why you're so keen on defending her.'

'I'm not, I was only trying to explain...'

But Jennie was no longer listening. 'Shall we carry on from where we left off', she said with a hopeful smirk.

They did so, though it soon became apparent to her that Derek's kisses lacked the warmth of his heart. When she commented on this, he replied with unnecessary frankness that the quality was bound to depreciate with someone as insatiable as herself.

Later he refused to accompany her back to the Hall on the ground of her father's ban on their meeting.

'But what he meant was that we shouldn't be seen about the town together', Jennie argued. 'Nobody's going to see us between here and the house.'

'You don't know. The police might suddenly arrive', he said obstinately. 'Apart from which,

I don't very much want to risk meeting your father at this moment.'

In the end Jennie had to be content with a half-promise that they would see each other again at the same spot the following afternoon. All things being equal, he had said, but he declined to specify in what way they might become so unequal as to prevent the meeting.

They parted with a short kiss, Jennie going off while Derek Yates stood thoughtfully smoking a cigarette until she and the dogs were out of sight and sound. Then moving carefully and avoiding the exposed part of the track, he set off in the same direction himself.


## CHAPTER FIVE

The events of Sunday can be shortly chronicled.

Jeremy and Sergeant Floyd both kept at their respective tasks; though Jeremy did so with a marked diffusion of effort as extraneous matters constantly thrust their way into his mind.

Hubert Waygood played a viciously contested game of croquet against a wisp of a woman with a gimlet eye.

Sylvia Ainsworth didn't stir outside her cottage all day.

Sir Geoffrey Rawlins wore a preoccupied expression and left his daughter to her own devices.

This suited Jennie well and in the afternoon she slipped out minus the dogs for her rendezvous with Derek Yates. Although he did turn up, it was not a satisfactory meeting. He appeared nervy and was so perfunctory in his manner that she returned to the house chafing in body and spirit.

In all, the day might be summed up as having reinforced an air of brooding which only a drastic purgative now seemed likely to dispel. One was to come.

★      ★      ★

Monday was the first working day of Seahaven Assizes and there was an early buzz of activity round the Town Hall which, besides housing the Assize court, contained municipal offices, the Mayor's parlour and, stuck on behind, the police station less the C.I.D. It was situated in a large square flanked at one end by the River Fran, on the far side of which were open meadows.

Like many an Assize court, Seahaven's, though of mild historical interest, was quite inadequate for its purpose. It was small and in design a combination of maze and cattle market. Advocates, court officials and even the public sat in numerous separate pens over the tops of which only their heads and shoulders showed. To go from one pen to an adjacent one invariably meant a move at least as complicated as that of a knight in a game of chess and could even involve a tiptoed exit through one creaking door of the court and a reappearance an instant later through another. Almost its only virtue was its freedom from noise and the only outside sound to penetrate was an occasional soothing one from the river.

The Coastal Circuit was one of the most popular among the judges, embracing as it did a number of pleasant seaside towns. In consequence it was usually bagged by a senior judge, particularly for the Summer Assizes. On this occasion it was Mr. Justice Dent who was adorning it with his presence. When at the Bar he'd been a practising member of the Circuit and he now took a fatherly and even proprietorial interest in its life.

This being the opening day of the Assize, the court was packed with people who were awaiting his lordship's arrival from the traditional service he'd been attending at St. Mary's Church across the square, at which the High Sheriff's chaplain had just prayed for his divine guidance with unflattering fervour. Suddenly there came wafting to those inside the uneasy sounds of a fanfare of trumpets. A few moments later the door behind the judge's seat was flung open, the tasselled curtain over it was pulled aside and Jeremy with everyone else in court stood up.

The scene that followed somewhat resembled the final curtain call of an amateur company in an over-ambitious production in a small village hall.

Mr. Justice Dent, impressive in full bottom wig and scarlet robe, stood in the centre with a faintly ironic expression on his face. Immediately to his right was Sir Geoffrey resplendent in his High Sheriff's outfit of black velvet swallow-tail jacket, black knee breeches, black silk stockings and black silver buckle shoes; but nevertheless managing to look at ease. Next to him stood his chaplain and then the Under-Sheriff, a small wizened local solicitor who wore morning dress and carried what looked like a white curtain rod but was in fact his wand of office. On the other side of the judge were his marshal, looking pink and flustered on this the first day of his first Assize as a judge's marshal, and his clerk who cast a practised and efficient eye over the scene.

Mr. Swinbank, the Clerk of Assize, turned in his seat just below the judge's and bowed to his lordship. There then followed his reading of several documents couched in archaic language, interspersed with more bowing and the doffing of a black tricorne hat which the judge suddenly produced from somewhere out of sight. At last it was all over and Mr. Justice Dent was vested with the necessary authority to preside at the

Assizes. Turning about with a certain air of relief, he disappeared through the door at the back of the bench, followed by his satellites.

It was five minutes before he reappeared, and by this time he had exchanged his full bottom wig for a short bobbed one and had shed part of his scarlet trimmings. He was now ready for work and jauntily carried his black cap (a mere oblong of folded silk) and a pair of white kid gloves in his right hand.

As soon as he was seated and had held a whispered colloquy with the Clerk of Assize, he fixed Jeremy with an amiable look and said:

'Yes, Mr. Harper, I understand you wish to make an application.'

'Er . . . yes, my lord. It concerns the case of Joseph Paxton, number six in your lordship's list. It's a contested case and I was wondering whether your lordship was likely to reach it today.'

'Who can tell, Mr. Harper, who can tell?' the judge said with bland unhelpfulness. 'However let me first ascertain a few basic facts. You, I take it, Mr. Harper, are appearing in the case?'

'Oh yes, my lord, I'm sorry, I'm defending.'

'Sorry you're defending, Mr. Harper?' echoed his lordship in mock surprise, chalking up his first little joke of the Assize.

'No, my lord. I mean I'm sorry that I had omitted to mention my part in the matter to your lordship.'

'It's as well I should know', observed the judge sunnily, having of course known all along. 'And naturally, Mr. Harper, you don't wish to hang around this Court when you could be more profitably occupied elsewhere—perhaps in the sunshine outside?'

Mr. Justice Dent had a large, smooth round face, a ridiculous button of a nose and a tiny mouth. At this point he peered at Jeremy over the top of his half-lens spectacles which looked in danger of toppling off the tip of his nose where they precariously perched. He was obviously enjoying himself and in no great hurry to get down to work. Though he may not have been as beloved of the Bar as he cared to imagine he was nevertheless popular with those members of it who practised on the Coastal Circuit. Amongst these it was generally conceded that he did try (and with moderate success) to remember his own first faltering steps in the profession.

Jeremy smiled with the requisite degree of sycophancy and continued to look earnestly towards his lordship.

An amiable if not nimble-witted young man, thought the judge, and paused to murmur as much to Sir Geoffrey sitting beside him.

'A local boy', the High Sheriff whispered back. 'Friend of my daughter's.'

The judge inclined his head with an air of polite interest and pondered, as he had had occasion to do before, the dangers of incautious observations to High Sheriffs. Some years previously he had made a brightly humorous aside concerning the colour of a certain lady's hair, only to discover later that she was the High Sheriff's aunt.

Perhaps the time had come to start doing what, according to the impressive documents so recently intoned by the Clerk of Assize, Her Majesty had despatched him to Seahaven to do. Namely to try prisoners and clear the gaol of those awaiting trial. The fact that most of them would probably return to it as men under sentence was neither here nor there. Leaning forward and poking a finger into Mr. Swinbank's wig, he held a whispered consultation with him. Then looking at Jeremy who was still standing hopefully before him, he said:

'I'll say that your case won't be taken before two o'clock, Mr. Harper.'

As he spoke he swept counsel's seats with a severe look as though in reproof of so much time-wasting.

Jeremy elbowed his way out of court. On his way to the barristers' robing-room, he met Sergeant Floyd and Hubert Waygood talking in the corridor. He was about to slip past them when Waygood called out to him.

'I had a word with the judge's clerk about that application of yours', he said importantly.

'Told him to tell the old boy to treat you gently', he added with a wink at Sergeant Floyd.

Jeremy assumed a dignified expression. It was insufferable, though, to be patronized in this way by someone who was a mere clerk. But Waygood had long since grown accustomed to regard himself as being 'of the profession', and with the outward sign of black jacket and striped trousers and all the inward assurance he did resemble one of the more mongrel barristers.

'How are you getting on with your inquiries into the robbery?' Jeremy asked Sergeant Floyd, turning an ostentatious shoulder on Waygood.

'O.K.; though there is one point on which you can enlighten me.' He paused and then said bleakly, 'What the hell were you doing in the park at the time?'

'Doing? I wasn't doing anything except going home.'

'That's what you said before; but it was right out of your way.'

'I agree it wasn't my direct route', Jeremy said with a shrug of indifference. 'It may even look a bit odd if you examine everything under a microscope, but I assure you there's really no mystery about it. It was a heavenly afternoon and I had no occasion to hurry home.' He was annoyed to note Sergeant Floyd's sceptical expression and to cover his discomfort said heartily, 'Well I hope you make an arrest soon. I imagine the longer it takes, the less chance there is of solving a case like this.'

Sergeant Floyd grunted non-committally.

'I must be getting along', Waygood said suddenly, as though the others had been unwarrantedly detaining him. 'We're snowed under with work in the office.'

The three men parted. As soon as Jeremy had disrobed, he went to phone Jennie but she was not at home.

\*     \*     \*

The case of *Regina* v. *Joseph Paxton* started promptly at two o'clock, Mr. Justice Dent's morning list having been a smooth succession of pleas of guilty so that by the time the court adjourned for lunch, only Jeremy's case remained outstanding.

On resumption of business in the afternoon, it was soon apparent that the judge had lost some of his geniality and was in a faintly peevish frame of mind. This was in fact due to a mild attack of indigestion, but unfortunately a judge can't even have a corn, let alone a heaving inside, without potential repercussions.

Prosecuting in Jeremy's case was a Mr. Pretty. He was a small blunt man who had somehow managed to get on without acquiring any of the Bar's more favoured mannerisms.

After Jeremy's client had pleaded not guilty in embarrassingly ringing tones, a jury was sworn to 'try the several issues joined between Our Sovereign Lady the Queen and the prisoner at the bar and a true verdict given according to the evidence'. Following this Mr. Pretty rose to his feet to open the case for the prosecution.

He hadn't got very far before Mr. Justice Dent, who had appeared absorbed in the papers before him, ostentatiously threw down his pencil, looked up and said irritably:

'Mr. Pretty, you have now informed the jury at least twice that it is the duty of the prosecution to satisy them as to the prisoner's guilt.'

Mr. Pretty cocked his head on one side and waited.

'That is so, is it not, Mr. Pretty?'

'Yes, my lord, I believe I have.'

The judge nodded meaningly, but Mr. Pretty remained mystified as was intended.

'I'm sorry, my lord. I don't quite follow . . .'

'For what purpose do you suppose *I* sit here?'

Asked by almost anyone other than a judge in court, this would be regarded as a somewhat incautious question; but judges can get away with such things.

'To . . . er . . . try the case, my lord', Mr. Pretty replied, hoping to have hit on the right answer.

'Yes, Mr. Pretty, precisely. To see fair play and to instruct the jury in the principles of law which they must apply to the fact in considering their verdict.' He paused to smother a burp and went on, 'You're there to prosecute, Mr. Pretty, not to usurp the judge's function. Oh, I know you did it to impress the jury with the Crown's Olympian lack of bias but you can do that, if you must, without stealing my lines.' He sat back in his seat with an air of infinite long-suffering. 'Yes, continue your opening, Mr. Pretty.'

The prosecution's case against his client was quickly deployed and proved to be as deadly as Jeremy had feared. All too soon came the moment he had been dreading: namely Paxton's arrival in the witness box. Early on, Jeremy had realized that he would be the type of witness to lead his counsel a merry dance before acrimoniously blaming him for the jury's verdict and the judge's sentence. Jeremy had tried to instil into him how important it was that he should make a favourable impression in the witness box and had given him certain advice on how to deport himself. He had known at the time, however, that Paxton didn't propose to pay the slightest heed to it and was bent on self-destruction.

Paxton now took the oath in the same spuriously self-righteous tone as that in which he had pleaded not quilty and awaited Jeremy's opening question.

'Is your full name Joseph Paxton?' Jeremy asked without enthusiasm.

'Yes, and may the good Lord above . . .'

'Kindly leave the deity out of your evidence', Mr. Justice Dent interrupted tartly.

'And do you live at 242 Bosnia Road, Seahaven, and are you a sales representative by occupation?' Jeremy went on hastily.

'I *did* live at number 242 once', Paxton said with a maddening smile. 'You see, that's where my ex-wife resides, but since I got my divorce decree last February . . .'

'Really, Mr. Harper, do we have to have your client's domestic life as well?'

'No, no, my lord.'

'Well then please try and control the witness.'

Jeremy fixed Paxton with the steeliest look he could muster and said:

'Now I want you to tell my lord and the jury when it was you first became connected with SUD?'

'Sud?' said the judge.

'Sud, m'lud', said Paxton cheerfully. 'The only washing powder that cleanses without sweat, toil or tears. Just sprinkle a little Sud into a bowl and . . .'

'Mr. Harper.' This time his lordship's tone was distinctly ominous. 'If you can't control your client in the box, he'll have to return to the dock. I'll not have the jury's time wasted with all this nonsense.'

'No, quite, my lord', Jeremy said, and looked beseechingly at Paxton. 'Please answer my questions and no more.'

'You must keep him on a shorter rein, Mr. Harper', the judge rumbled on peevishly. 'Questions like your last are an invitation to trouble.'

'Yes, my lord.'

Although this was not Jeremy's first blooding at the hands of a High Court judge, it *was* his first in his home town, which made it worse.

Throughout the recent verbal skirmish, Sir Geoffrey Rawlins had sat with a forbiddingly stern expression; though Jeremy had been relieved to note that this did not appear to be connected with events in court. Indeed he had showed no sign of following the proceedings with any attention at all.

Sylvia had come into court during the last few minutes and had sat down next to Mr. Swinbank to whom she had handed a sheaf of documents. Jeremy felt that she was somehow with him in his harried state. There was a sympathetic look in her eyes that brought him a grain of much-needed comfort. Hubert Waygood on the other hand wasn't bothering to hide his smirk as he leant against the far end of the jury box. In some uncanny way he had contrived, as always, to be in court when counsel was at the receiving end of the flying grapeshot.

Jeremy was in the process of composing what he prayed would be an unfaulted question when the door behind the judge's seat unexpectedly opened and a police inspector stepped forward and whispered into Sir Geoffrey's ear. As he did so, the High Sheriff's features froze into an expression of glacial fury. After appearing to hesitate for a second, he got up and followed the officer out.

The incident managed to create a moment of palpable tension and it was with considerable relief that Jeremy heard the judge say:

'I think we'll adjourn for a quarter of an hour. It's been a tiring afternoon and I'm sure the jury will be glad of a short break.' Turning toward them he went on, 'If you retire to your room, members of the jury, some tea will be brought to you. I've arranged that as I thought you'd probably welcome a little refreshment at this stage of your duties.'

'Artful old buffer', Waygood muttered into Jeremy's ear as judge and jury filed out of court. 'Now, when he comes to tell them what a villain your bloke is, they'll accept it without demur. Anything from such a kind, considerate judge must be gospel.'

Jeremy made a non-committal throat noise and turned away, pretending to busy himself with his papers.

Later he went out for a soothing cigarette.

It was when Mr. Justice Dent was on the point of returning to Court that the news broke.

Looking more self-important than ever, Waygood came across to the end of counsel's row where Jeremy was sitting and, dropping his voice, said dramatically:

'I've just heard they've made an arrest in Friday's robbery job. You'll never guess...'

Jeremy felt Waygood's eyes boring into him and his mind leapt immediately to Sir Geoffrey's sudden exit from court. Drops of ice cold perspiration started to trickle from his armpits and yet he couldn't bring himself to ask the obvious question.

'Yates', Waygood said with relish and scuttled away.

## CHAPTER SIX

In due course Derek Yates appeared before the local Magistrates charged with stealing the sum of eight thousand pounds, the property of his employer. After a certain amount of technical fuss and bother, he was committed to stand trial at the adjourned Seahaven Assizes to which Mr. Justice Dent would be returning in about a month's time.

The hearing of the case in the Magistrates'

Court lasted only a morning and there was no cross-examination of any of the prosecution witnesses. In reserving his cross-examination defending counsel made it plain, however, that the charge would be fought tooth and nail at the Assizes and that Yates, who had made none of the usual damaging admissions, had a complete answer which he would put forward at the proper time.

On this challenging note the curtain had come down on Act I of the drama and Yates had returned to Franwich prison to await Act II; though not before the closing stages of the Magistrates' hearing had become charged with acrimony. This had been generated by Sergeant Floyd's strenuous opposition to defending counsel's application for bail.

After Mr. Gilvray (for it was he who had been briefed to appear on behalf of Yates) had made a most pressing plea which Floyd had baldly opposed, there ensued the following dialogue.

'Why do you oppose bail, officer?'

'Because I think the prisoner will abscond.'

'What evidence have you got to support that theory?'

'It isn't based on evidence.'

'Merely on police prejudice?'

'Certainly not.'

'What then?'

'We've not been able to trace a single penny of this money and . . .'

'If you charge an innocent man, how can you expect to find the money?'

There was no answer to this and the two protagonists stood glaring at each other. In the dock, Yates sat leaning forward intently, his chin cupped in his hands, the pallor on his face accentuated by contrast with his neatly-trimmed black moustache. A picture, indeed, of anxious expectancy. Mr. Gilvray pounded away once more.

'I put it to you that your opposition to bail in this case is monstrously unfair?'

'You can put it how you like.'

'Don't be impertinent, officer.'

Sergeant Floyd merely shrugged his shoulders.

'My client has completely denied the charge on every possible occasion, has he not?'

'Yes.'

'Not one word of admission have you been able to wring out of him?'

'I haven't tried to wring any admissions out of him and I resent your suggestion.'

Glaring harder than ever, Mr. Gilvray gathered himself together for a final assault.

'Is a certain well-known and influential local citizen the moving spirit behind this opposition to my client's bail?' he asked, adding recklessly, 'I'm quite prepared to name the gentleman if you wish.'

At this point the Magistrates' Clerk had

hurriedly intervened and after a brief consultation amongst themselves, the Magistrates had rejected Mr. Gilvray's application, to the sound of that gentleman's angry, muttered comments.

The four weeks that elapsed before Yates's trial were peculiarly calm and did nothing to foretell the storm that was brewing.

## CHAPTER SEVEN

On the day before the trial opened, Detective-Sergeant Floyd drove over to Franwich prison to have a talk with the Chief Officer there, who was expecting him.

'I'm afraid you're in for a disappointment', the prison officer said when they were seated in a small, sunless room which smelt strongly of disinfectant. 'Apart from his solicitor, the only person to visit him has been Miss Rawlins. She's been here three times, but of course there's always been someone present when she's seen him and certainly nothing suspicious has ever happened.'

'What used they to talk about?' Floyd asked.

'She did most of the talking always: about what they'd do when he was acquitted and that sort of thing. He usen't to say much. In fact, he hasn't taken very kindly to his enforced stay here. Fretted a lot, he has.'

'And what about the interviews with his solicitor?'

'You don't suspect him, do you?'

'No, but Yates might have tried to use him innocently, to smuggle a message out.'

'Of course even prison routine is subject to the human element', the Chief Officer said with a pout. 'But I *can* tell you that we've kept our eyes and ears extra wide open and there's been absolutely nothing to arouse any suspicions.' There was a silence and then he added, 'I take it you were hoping for some clue to the whereabouts of the money.'

'Yes; but it seems I must look elsewhere. Thanks, anyway.'

Up at Seahaven Hall that evening, there was an atmosphere of acute friction. Sir Geoffrey and Jennie had spent the whole of dinner arguing from behind their respectively entrenched positions, with the result that by the time the meal was over Jennie had reached a state of flaring resentment against her father, and he of autocratic unreasonableness toward her.

'That's my final word, Jennie. I absolutely forbid you to appear in court during Yates's trial.'

'And what do you think people are going to say about your sitting there next to the judge dressed up like Little Lord Fauntleroy?'

'That has nothing to do with it. And, in any event, as High Sheriff I have no alternative but to attend.'

'I believe you want to be there', she said defiantly. 'Yes, I honestly believe you hope Derek will be sent to prison for something he's never done.'

Sir Geoffrey's expression was one of cold distaste as he studied his daughter.

'You're talking nonsense', he said. 'The truth is—and it's time you were told it—that you've worked yourself up into believing he's in love with you when everything points the other way. He doesn't care an unripe fig for you. All he was ever interested in was the money he thought he'd get by marrying you. Once he saw how the land lay, he couldn't drop you quickly enough.'

As he spoke, Jennie stared at him with wide-eyed ferocity.

'That's not true', she burst out. 'And what's more we'll soon prove it to you—prove it in a way you won't like. You shan't wreck my life.'

Sir Geoffrey let his monocle fall from his eye and made as if to go.

'I believe you don't want me to go near the trial for quite a different reason', she continued, flinging the words at his back.

He paused and turned.

'Yes? Go on', he said quietly.

'I think you're frightened I may learn

something about the case that you don't want me to know. That's the real reason you're keeping me away: not because of what people might say.'

He eyed her curiously and then said:

'In your present mood, I can hardly hope to persuade you that my sole wish is to save us both from as much embarrassment as possible.' He spoke with an air of forbearance, his anger seeming suddenly to have melted and left him weary of the quarrel.

But Jennie's only reaction was to regard him with patent suspicion.

★      ★      ★

'''Morning, Sylvia', Mr. Swinbank said as he entered the large office in the Town Hall which he and his staff used during the Assizes.

The greeting was addressed at Sylvia's anatomy as she bent over one of the huge hampers out of which they lived on circuit. She straightened up.

'Good morning, Mr. Swinbank', she replied in little above a whisper.

'I say, you all right today?' he asked anxiously. 'You look a bit under the weather.'

'I didn't sleep very well last night and I've got rather a headache, but I'll be O.K.'

'I hope so', Mr. Swinbank said fervently as he gazed round the paper-laden tables and fished a small crumpled bag of boiled sweets out of his pocket. He bought a fresh supply each morning on his way to court and sucked them non-stop throughout the day. Occasionally as a mark of real approbation, he would offer one to the person with whom he happened to be talking. But this was rare. He went on, 'The Yates case shouldn't last long and then we've finished and you can take a nice long rest.'

He turned to hang up his umbrella and battered black homburg behind the door.

'Hasn't Waygood turned up yet?' he asked as he removed his soft collar and took a stiff winged one from the japanned box in which he kept the smaller items, including wig, of his court apparel.

'I haven't seen him.'

'Tiresome fellow, he is. Always bustling but never at the right time and place.' He disappeared into the small closet which adjoined the office and continued to talk, though his voice was partially drowned by the noise of gushing taps and gurgling waste-pipes. 'Is he still paying you assiduous court?' Before Sylvia had time to reply, he appeared in the doorway, towel in hand. 'Waygood, I mean?'

She turned away with a half-shrug of annoyance.

'Oh, he's very fond of you', he went on unabashed. 'Give him half a chance and you'd be Mrs. Waygood in no time.'

'Really!'

'I mean it and he means it even more. Don't underestimate the heart that beats in that wiry little frame. Our Hubert rather fancies himself...'

'You don't have to tell me that', Sylvia broke in.

Further exchange of views was forestalled by the arrival of the subject himself.

''Morning all', Waygood said breezily, removing Mr. Swinbank's hat to a broken peg and carefully hanging his own where it had been. Then rubbing his hands together, he walked over to his desk. 'All set? Should be an interesting case. Think I'll try and pop into court this morning. Nothing special for me to do in the office, is there?'

The question was rhetorical. Normally he and Sylvia slipped in and out of court maintaining a general liaison between Mr. Swinbank, who was anchored there, and the office. When work in the office was slack, however, it was not unusual for them to sit in court if there was a case of sufficient interest.

'No, I can manage here on my own', Sylvia said, quickly.

*    *    *

Outwardly Mr. Justice Dent looked the same as he had a month earlier. Inwardly he was jaded and feeling in need of the vacation which he would already have been enjoying but for this tiresome return to his starting-point. However, he didn't intend to waste undue time trying what looked to him to be a straightforward issue of fact in the Yates case. He had read the depositions (the written record of evidence given at the Magistrates' Court) and had made up his mind to pass a severe sentence if the fellow was convicted. He would soon find out where such brazen and impudent conduct led. So ran the judge's thoughts as Mr. Swinbank read out the indictment and the jury was sworn.

Unlike Jeremy's recent client at Seahaven Assizes, Derek Yates pleaded not guilty with just the right degree of firm-toned sincerity. Indeed his whole bearing radiated an aura of unquestionable innocence.

Mr. Pretty had been briefed to prosecute and Mr. Gilvray again appeared for the defence.

As soon as Mr. Pretty rose to his feet to begin his opening speech, Mr. Swinbank sat thankfully back and after careful selection popped a cherry-coloured sweet into his mouth.

In simple, unglamorous language Mr. Pretty told the jury what the case was about. He related the events surrounding the supposed robbery and stated that the prosecution's evidence could only lead to the conclusion that it, the robbery, had been faked. He concluded his opening address by stressing a number of inconsistencies in Yates's various accounts of the affair and these, he suggested, showed it to be no less than a cleverly and carefully devised plan to defraud his employer of eight thousand pounds.

The first main witness for the prosecution was the driver of the car that had taken Yates to the bank both on the day in question and the previous week when Yates also alleged that they had been followed. Towards the end of his examination-in-chief, Mr. Pretty asked:

'On either of these occasions did you yourself notice anything suspicious?'

'Can't really say I did.'

'Did you on either occasion notice any car following you?'

'No, I don't think so.'

'I don't know what you mean by *think*', Mr. Justice Dent broke in testily. 'Either you did notice a car following you or you did not.'

'No, that's what I mean; I don't think I did.'

'The jury want to know whether you did or you did not', the judge said in a grating tone.

'I can't say I did.'

'So you didn't see any car following you on either occasion?'

'No, I don't think so.'

His lordship gave the witness a withering look and with a theatrical sigh leant back and closed his eyes.

Mr. Pretty sat down and Mr. Gilvray was

immediately on his feet hurling his first question.

'You're not saying, are you, that no car followed you?'

'On which occasion?' The judge asked, his eyelids snapping up like roller blinds.

'Either?' said Mr. Gilvray, equally briskly.

'No, how can I?' the witness replied in a puzzled tone. 'I was driving. I don't know whether *you've* ever driven along High Street when there's traffic about. You have to keep your eyes to the front, not fixed out of the rear window.'

'Precisely', Mr. Gilvray said in a satisfied tone. 'So that there could have been a car following you in the way the accused says?'

'Yes, I suppose so.'

'You had no reason to doubt the accused's word about that?'

'Why should I doubt his word?'

'I'm saying you had no reason to, that's correct, isn't it?'

'I don't follow you.'

Once more Mr. Justice Dent took over and with heavily forced patience said:

'Did you or did you not—not that it seems to me to have any relevance—believe the accused when he told you that he thought your car was being followed?'

'Which time?'

'On either of the two occasions?'

'Why shouldn't I have believed him?'

'Did you?' the judge almost shouted.

'I suppose so.'

'But you yourself never noticed anything suspicious?'

'What sort of thing do you mean?'

By this time it was apparent that the witness had reached a state of almost pathological suspicion of everyone in court.

'Cars following you?'

'I never saw any.'

'At last! At last we've got it: you never saw any car following you in a suspicious manner.'

'No, I don't think so.'

At this, Mr. Justice Dent threw down his pencil with such a violent show of exasperation that Mr. Swinbank inadvertently swallowed his sweet and had to drink a hasty glass of water to dislodge it from his throat.

Several further efforts were made to coax something positive out of the witness, but finally he was allowed to retire from the scene as frustrated by the law's pettifogging obtuseness as the law was by his inability to fit tidily into its ways.

The next witness was Jeremy, who approached the witness box as if it might have been the scaffold. Once arrived, he peered about him with near-panic. The whole court looked bewilderingly different from this angle and he felt separated by a great unbridgeable

gulf from counsel's homely bench. He stumbled
through the oath like a tyro and braced himself
for Mr. Pretty's first question.

'Is your name Jeremy Harper and are you a
barrister-at-law?' Mr. Pretty asked, looking at
Jeremy as though he had never seen him before.

Jeremy nodded.

'Please answer yes or no.'

Jeremy fought down the urge to giggle and
say 'no'.

'Yes', he replied, meekly.

He became suddenly aware that Mr. Justice
Dent appeared to be larger than usual and was
alarmingly close. Moreover, he was able to see
much more of his lordship than he was
accustomed to from counsels' seats. It was all
most disconcerting and made Jeremy feel as
conspicuous as a pork chop on a vegetarian
menu.

After he had answered three more questions,
the judge turned and surveyed him in a most
disquieting manner. Mr. Pretty could see that
something was in the air and metaphorically
waved the judge on.

'Mr. Harper', Mr. Justice Dent began in a
sad, reproachful tone, 'I wonder how many
times in this court you have been exasperated
by witnesses who won't keep their voices up.'
He blinked at Jeremy over the top of his
spectacles and went on, 'And yet it seems to
have profited you nothing. So far, your

evidence has amounted to no more than a series of mumbles out of which I haven't caught a word. I'm quite sure the jury can't have either', he concluded. 'Do try and speak up, Mr. Harper. You have a pleasant speaking voice: don't deprive us of it.'

Jeremy blushed furiously.

'I'm sorry, my lord', he murmured and then glowered as he caught a broad wink from Waygood who was smirking at him from the seat beside Mr. Swinbank.

Squaring his shoulders, he turned to meet Mr. Pretty's next question. As he did so his eye caught that of Yates, sitting forward in the small box-like dock and watching him with ferociously greedy attention. It was obvious from the dark shadows beneath his eyes and the slight tick at the corner of one of the lids that he was under a desperate strain. His train of thought brought Jeremy's wandering glance round to Sir Geoffrey. The High Sheriff was sitting on the far side of the judge from the witness-box and was leaning right back, thoroughly relaxed as he gently massaged the palms of his hands along the smooth, wooden arms of his chair. There was something vaguely sinister about the movement: something indicative of the man's power, and Jeremy looked away with a slight shiver.

From the outset, Jeremy had regarded his evidence as being relatively neutral: of little assistance to the prosecution and of no great concern to the defence. It amounted in fact to corroboration of Yates's own explanation of the affair—an explanation which the prosecution set out to prove false, and it was useful to that end in so far as it pegged Yates down.

Mr. Pretty and Mr. Gilvray each saw in him, however, the witness from whom it might be possible to lure some tiny but telling detail which would strengthen his own case or weaken the opponent's. Thus, after Mr. Pretty had elicited from him the main facts of what had happened on that fateful Friday afternoon, he asked:

'Mr. Harper, just tell the jury this. Did *you* see any signs of robbers in the vicinity of the park?'

'No, I didn't see anyone at all', Jeremy said and then quickly added, 'except I should explain that I wasn't expecting to see anyone of course.'

'Or hear any suspicious noises?'

'No-o.'

'What species of suspicious noises are you suggesting, Mr. Pretty?' the judge interposed.

'People running? Cars racing away? That sort of thing?'

'No, but I should like to add that . . .'

'You heard nothing of that sort?' Mr. Pretty broke in.

'No; except to be absolutely fair I must make

71

it clear that I wasn't on the look-out for any of the things you mention.'

'I have long observed', said the judge, addressing the court at large, 'that lawyers in the witness box do all those things which as advocates they exhort witnesses not to do. They qualify everything they say and usually prefer to answer any question but that asked.' He beamed at Jeremy who returned him a sickly smile.

Mr. Pretty waited a suitable time for all to enjoy his lordship's sally before going on. Then he asked:

'Does it follow that everything was extremely quiet and peaceful?'

'That's a grossly leading question', protested Mr. Gilvray, springing to his feet.

'It seemed the logical conclusion from what the witness had previously said', Mr. Pretty retorted unabashed.

'My learned friend's job is to ask proper questions, not put so-called logical conclusions into the witness's mouth.'

Mr. Justice Dent looked up slowly and brought his mind back from the trout stream where it had temporarily drifted.

'Yes, go on, Mr. Pretty', he said, 'but try not to offend Mr. Gilvray any more.'

By now Jeremy was beginning to get his witness legs and was quite enjoying the role. It was ridiculous to say, as was often said and as the judge had recently implied, that lawyers made bad witnesses. One had only to tell the truth and it was plainer than plain sailing. Trouble was that too many witnesses failed to tell the *whole* truth for one reason or another.

'I beg your pardon, would you mind repeating the question', he stammered, suddenly aware that Mr. Pretty was staring at him for an answer.

'I asked you whether you think you would have seen or heard a car driving away if there had been one.'

'Another objectionable question', Mr. Gilvray said hotly. 'In the first place there is no evidence of the existence of any car and in the second, how can the witness possibly say whether or not he might have heard something when in fact he has told us that he heard nothing?'

The judge sighed and looked towards Jeremy.

'Mr. Harper, as I understand the topography, there is only one road at that end of the park and you were by the park entrance?'

'Yes, my lord.'

'And while you were there, you didn't see or hear any motor-cars?'

'No, my lord.'

'Does that satisfy you?' he asked looking at both counsel together.

'I'm much obliged, my lord', said Mr. Pretty.

Mr. Gilvray said:

'Yes, my lord; though it doesn't prove that there was no car in the vicinity.'

'That'll be for the jury to decide', Mr. Justice Dent said firmly.

Soon after this, Mr. Pretty sat down and Mr. Gilvray rose to cross-examine. If counsel for the prosecution had treated Jeremy as a stranger, counsel for the defence, it soon became apparent, proposed to regard him as a personal foe.

'Now, Mr. Harper', he said, giving his gown a good tug about his shoulders, 'let's have no beating about the bush. Because you never saw the men who robbed Yates, that doesn't mean they didn't exist, does it?'

'No-o.'

'And Yates never said they had a car, did he?'

'No; but we didn't . . .'

'Robbers need not necessarily move by car even in this petrol-driven age, huh?'

'I think that's a comment rather than a question', Jeremy replied, and Mr. Gilvray coloured up as he observed the judge nod in sardonic agreement. Right, he'd show Harper it didn't pay to be clever in the witness box.

'What exactly were you doing hanging around outside the Queen Elizabeth park on the day in question?' he asked in an unpleasant tone.

'I wasn't hanging about at all', Jeremy replied

hotly. 'I was on my way home.'

'On your way home?'

'Yes. I know it wasn't my direct route but that's where I was going.'

Mr. Gilvray waited a moment. Then he asked, cocking an eyebrow at Jeremy,

'Do you prefer not to tell the court why you were going home by such a devious route?'

'There's nothing to tell', Jeremy replied, stung by the unfair implication of the question.

'But there you just happened to be, outside the park gate at the time of the robbery?' Mr. Gilvray's tone was venomously sarcastic.

Jeremy glared and felt his cheeks burning. He was being cross-examined in a grossly unfair manner and no one was lifting a finger to protect him. Now he understood why witnesses often went to such lengths to avoid getting caught up in any legal process. And what happened to those who were sufficiently public-spirited to come forward? They were kept waiting about endlessly at great personal inconvenience, and when at last they did reach the witness box they were immediately made to feel ridiculous, if not actual liars. Everything was heavily weighted in favour of their legal inquisitors who harried them with unfair questions and showed a masterly skill in asking the most obtuse ones. After all, who better than the witness himself knew what he should say? But was he allowed to? On no account. He had to confine himself under pain of stern judicial censure to answering questions put, for the most part, in a quite unanswerable form.

It was with a sense of fierce resentment that Jeremy, the witness, eventually stepped down and made way for Detective-Sergeant Floyd.

Floyd was as used to giving evidence as he was to cleaning his teeth. Awkward questions bounced off him like rubber balls off a granite rock and he always contrived to say all he wanted to, regardless of what he was asked.

By the time Mr. Pretty had completed his examination-in-chief, no one in court could be in the slightest doubt that he, Sergeant Floyd, was firmly convinced of Yates's guilt and was determined to see justice done.

The prosecution's case had consisted of numerous small but significant pieces of evidence designed to prove the utter improbability of Yates's description of events. Their sum effect was to show that, if his story was true, then the robbers could only have departed from the scene by supernatural means. And that, it was hoped, would be too much even for a Seahaven jury to swallow.

Mr. Gilvray in his cross-examination tried to destroy the effect of Floyd's evidence by suggesting that it was thoroughly tendentious and unworthy of belief. Finally he asked:

'You have never traced a single penny of the money, have you?'

'No.'

'Have you searched the park for it?'

'Yes.'

'Are you satisfied that the eight thousand pounds must have left the park before you arrived on the scene?'

'Yes.'

'How?'

'How?' Floyd echoed.

'Yes, how if not via the men who robbed Yates?'

'By an accomplice of course.'

'But you've no evidence of any accomplice.'

'Not as to his identity. But I know there was one', Floyd replied in a flint-like tone.

The court rippled with muted excitement and all eyes turned expectantly towards the man in the dock.

Only Sergeant Floyd watched elsewhere.

## CHAPTER EIGHT

When the trial was resumed the following morning, Yates was at once called to give evidence.

Vacating the dock by a small door at the rear, he made his tortuous way to the witness box which stood like a small bulbous pulpit on the end of a narrow pier. There he waited erect and motionless until bidden to take the oath, which he did with an impressive degree of sincerity.

While he awaited Mr. Gilvray's first question, he permitted himself a quick glance round the assembled company. Jeremy sitting over on the far side of the court studiously avoided his look. Sir Geoffrey with head cocked on one side and a petulant expression was being whispered to by the Under-Sheriff. A faintly sardonic smile flickered across Yates's features as his gaze passed on to Hubert Waygood and Sylvia Ainsworth sitting below him. Finally it swept across to Sergeant Floyd who, he found, was watching him intently. By the time the first question came he had satisfied himself that Jennie was nowhere in court.

As Yates's evidence came to be extracted from him, Mr. Gilvray soon realized that he could never hope to hear a better witness in his own behalf. He once more gave his account of events and one had the impression that he was reliving them detail by detail, urged on only by Mr. Gilvray's occasional 'Yes, and then?' or 'What happened next?'

When he reached the crucial point, Mr. Gilvray held up an admonitory hand.

'Now Yates I want you to be very careful about this next part of your evidence. I want you to tell the jury exactly where you were when you first saw or heard the men, and where they came from. Do you follow? Don't omit a single detail.'

Yates nodded, managing to look like the teacher's favourite pupil, and turning towards the jury said:

'I was walking along this path through the park. I don't know whether you know it, but there are fairly thick bushes and trees on each side. I had just reached a point by a lilac tree and these men must have been hiding behind it because I suddenly heard a slight rustling sound to my right and as I turned they sort of came straight at me.' He paused to draw breath and went on, 'I never really saw them; just a blur of movement and . . .' He broke off again and said apologetically, 'I'm afraid it's not very easy to explain clearly in words. I wonder . . .' Here he turned towards his counsel. 'I wonder if I might show the jury a small sketch I've drawn. I think it might help them to follow my evidence.'

'Let me see it', Mr. Gilvray said. After scrutinizing it, he passed it up to Mr. Justice Dent. 'Perhaps this might be made an exhibit, my lord.'

The judge examined it with a supercilious air and then held it up at arm's length as if it might be something out of the gutter.

'I suppose so if you wish, Mr. Gilvray, but I can't see that it's going to assist anyone very much. In any event don't let's waste undue time over it.' He let it flutter down on to the Clerk of Assize's desk. 'Give it an exhibit number and then show it to the jury.'

'It'll be exhibit six', said Mr. Swinbank, scribbling this on the top of it and handing it to the usher who fed it in at one end of the jury box and then hurried to the other to await its arrival there. Meanwhile twelve pairs of willing eyes studied it with expressions ranging from blank incomprehension to obvious disappointment.

As it passed from juror to juror, Yates observed its unenthusiastic reception with apparent dismay. It seemed he had pinned hopes on its ability to open the jury's eyes to the truth of his evidence. When it was finally returned to the Clerk's desk, Waygood shoved it under a pile of papers in front of Sylvia, who was engrossed in a whispered conversation with one of the office staff.

Yates said:

'I wonder if I might have my sketch again ...' It was handed back to him and holding it up rather like a lecturer, he went on, 'This X marks where the men must have been hiding—behind that bush by the lilac tree.'

'What sort of bush?' asked Mr. Gilvray.

'I'm afraid I'm not sure. It was a bushy sort of bush.'

'Most helpful', the judge said acidly. 'But really, Mr. Gilvray, does it matter whether these supposed robbers were behind this bush, that bush or the other bush. The prisoner has told us they were hiding somewhere near the path and he's produced a sketch. Isn't that sufficient?'

'Yes, my lord, with respect I agree. I don't think we need go into further detail.' Addressing himself to Yates, Mr. Gilvray added, 'Have you now finished with the sketch?'

'Yes if I've managed to make it clear what the relevant positions were. You see I can pinpoint them because that particular lilac tree is different from the others...'

'Yes, very well', Mr. Gilvray broke in before his client could further antagonize the judge. But it seemed that Mr. Justice Dent was now being tried from a different quarter.

'Before you go on, Mr. Gilvray, perhaps we could have a little quiet. There seems to be an endless conversation going on below me. Would its participants very much mind conducting it elsewhere?'

In the sudden silence that followed, Sylvia blushed a deep beetroot colour, the judge's rebuke having been supplemented by an unnecessarily obvious nudge from Waygood. Wishing she could dissolve, she tiptoed out of court. When she returned a quarter of an hour later, Yates was being cross-examined.

Mr. Pretty's method of cross-examination was a plodding one and though it quite often achieved its end, this never for one moment seemed likely.

'The truth is that your evidence is a tissue of lies from beginning to end, is it not?' he asked in a matter-of-fact tone.

'No, it's the truth.'

'Let us see, then.'

They did so in laborious detail and at the end nothing fresh had emerged. Yates stuck to what he had said and even counter-attacked by suggesting that the apparent weaknesses in his evidence were really its strength.

'If I'd invented all this, as you allege, I could surely have made the story a good deal stronger.'

Later, this was seized on by Mr. Gilvray in his closing address to the jury. The truthful witness, he said, is not one who has a slick and ready answer to everything. Indeed, is it not the latter who arouses our suspicions by a surfeit of plausibility? he asked rhetorically and went on to point out the absence of any motive. Yates, he said, had a good steady job as cashier at Rawlins Paper Mills Ltd.; he was not in debt and he had no financial worries of any sort. Why then should he do anything as criminal and crazy as to steal eight thousand pounds of his firm's wages? On the other hand, he reminded the jury, there had recently been a considerable number of similarly audacious robberies and what was more probable than that this was another, devised and plotted by the same brain, the same master-mind as had been behind the earlier ones? (The public gallery had experienced a tingle of excitement at this further hint of a mysterious grey eminence.)

There was no doubt that it was a fine rousing jury speech and if a snap verdict had been returned on its completion, it would unhesitatingly have been in Yates's favour.

Such, however, is frequently the case; but the moment for verdicts hadn't arrived and there had first to come a cold, astringent dose of judicial direction.

Mr. Justice Dent summed up carefully and fairly, after which the jury retired for two hours and twenty minutes before returning their verdict of—'guilty'.

His lordship appeared neither pleased nor surprised and listened impassively to Mr. Gilvray's plea in mitigation. Then addressing the prisoner in a tone of complete detachment he said:

'Derek Yates, the jury have found you guilty of robbing your employer of a very large sum of money. By implication they have also found you guilty of an impudent and lying defence. *I* don't propose to waste any words on you. The sentence of the court is that you be imprisoned for five years.'

With grim expression Yates listened and then as the two prison officers motioned him to disappear down the steps which led to the cells, he swept the court with a blazing stare, letting it come to final rest on Sir Geoffrey who might have been waiting for it and met it unflinchingly.

There was a moment of agonizing tension before he turned like an automaton and was hustled out of sight.


# CHAPTER NINE

Sylvia opened the door of the office and let out a small gasp of surprise.

'Hello', said Sergeant Floyd with a crooked smile. 'Sorry if I startled you, but since you weren't here I thought I'd try and find what I was looking for myself. I was going to leave you a little note. I knew you couldn't be far away as the door wasn't locked.'

'I went out for a cup of tea', she said dully. She looked tired and even bemused and remained standing just inside the door.

'I came for that cheque book which was an exhibit in the Smythe case', Floyd said. 'The owner would like it back and now that Smythe's application for leave to appeal has been dismissed, I thought it might be returned to him.'

Sylvia walked across to one of the huge hampers and pulled out a large stiff envelope.

From this she extracted a crumpled cheque book and handed it to Floyd.

'Thanks. Yes, this is it', he said. He looked at her curiously. 'I'd get on home if I were you. You don't look too well.'

For a second it seemed that she was going to speak, but instead she turned away and started toying with some papers on her desk.

'It's half past six', he went on, looking at his watch, 'and everyone else seems to have knocked off.' All indeed was still and silent, the Town Hall having been surrendered into the care of its night watchman who at that moment was sinking a second bottle of beer to help sustain him through the dark hours ahead. 'What did you think of the result in the Yates case?' he asked after a pause. Was it his imagination or did she suddenly go tense at the question?

'What do you mean?' she countered without looking round.

'Were you surprised at the verdict?'

'Who is ever surprised at anything a Seahaven jury does?'

'I'd have been if they'd acquitted in this case. Well, all that now remains is to catch his accomplice.'

'Yes?' Sylvia said, still keeping her back turned on him.

'And my bet is that when we do, it'll fair shake this town. It might even prove to be a seven-day wonder.'

'Have you any ideas ...?' she asked hesitantly.

'Wait and see.'

'Of course being mysterious is a favourite police gambit, isn't it? You must never let on how little you really know.'

Her tone was strangely dispassionate and robbed the words of the sarcasm they otherwise imparted. Sergeant Floyd stared at her in thoughtful silence. Suddenly he said:

'Did you notice the look Yates gave old Rawlins as he was leaving the dock? He's a tough one is Sir Geoffrey. Wonder what he's telling his daughter now.' He paused and in a friendly tone continued, 'Of course you've known the family since you were a child, haven't you? In fact I suppose you and Jennie Rawlins almost grew up together?'

'Hardly that. My mother was Miss Jennie's nurse, but I was away at school most of the time. And then after mother retired and we moved into the cottage, we scarcely ever went up to the Hall, though mother did go and help when Lady Rawlins was so ill just before she died. But I haven't set foot inside there in the past two years. It's entirely thanks to Sir Geoffrey, however, that I have a home at all', she added with seeming irrelevance. 'Miss Jennie and I don't have much in common, though. I have to earn my living.' It was quite a speech and when she had finished she turned abruptly back to her desk, making it clear she wished him to leave. He did so.

After he had gone, she locked the door on the inside, slumped into a chair and stared with unseeing eyes across the room. It was quite some time before she got up and with slow and painful movements collected her things and left.

★      ★      ★

Later that same evening Jeremy went up to the Hall. He had earlier phoned Jennie the result of the case and she had asked him to come along after dinner.

As he accelerated up the drive, he pondered over her reaction to the situation. She had received the news of her fiancé's conviction calmly: there had been neither outburst nor hysterical breakdown. 'I see', had been all that she had said and she had thanked him for calling her.

He found her out on the lawn with the dogs and she waited for him to come over to where she was standing.

'Let's go for a stroll', she said, linking an arm through his and heading towards where the lawn tapered into a narrow sward between two copses.

'Has your father come back yet?'

She nodded.

'He was in for dinner. He's being very sweet and sympathetic. I suppose he now thinks he can afford to be.'

From what she went on to say, Jeremy gathered that Sir Geoffrey must have given his daughter a carefully edited version of the court proceedings in an endeavour to spare her feelings.

'How long would five years mean in practice?' she asked.

'Three years and eight months. One-third is the maximum remission for good conduct.'

'And how soon will it be before his appeal is heard?'

'That depends, but perhaps he won't appeal. I mean he may be advised not to.'

Jennie stared at him incredulously.

'Not appeal? But of course he will. They're bound to squash his sentence.'

'Quash', Jeremy said mechanically and went on, 'I wouldn't bank on that. The Court of Criminal Appeal don't normally interfere with jury's verdicts unless there's been a substantial misdirection in law by the judge.'

Jennie suddenly halted in her tracks and Jeremy noticed how pale she had gone.

'But they must let him off', she said with a touch of hysteria.

It had never occurred to Jeremy she might be hanging all her hopes on such a possibility. No wonder she had taken things so calmly up to this moment. But now there was every sign of a scene and Jeremy was filled with apprehension.

'Come on, let's go as far as Piglet Ridge', he said, putting out a coaxing hand; but she stood rigidly obstinate.

'So that's why Daddy was sweet and kind to me when he came back. He reckoned it was now all over for good between me and Derek.'

'Come on, Jennie', Jeremy said, with increasing anxiety.

'Well, I'll show everyone', she went on, ignoring him. 'What's more, I'll wait three years and eight months if I have to. *If* I have to.'

There was something overwhelmingly provocative in her stance, her expression and her tone, and Jeremy experienced sudden streaking pangs of jealousy. In the next instant he had pulled her roughly to him and was kissing her with savage abandon. His deep yearning for her, which he had so long kept submerged beneath a conventional veneer, had volcanically erupted.

When at last he released her passive body, she turned and stumbled from him with choking sobs.

★ ★ ★

Still this same evening, Hubert Waygood decided to propose to Sylvia. The summer term was all but over and the propinquity of the past two months would shortly end when he went north to stay with his sister for the long vacation.

This, therefore, he reasoned, was the propitious moment and success was confidently envisaged.

The rebuff which he received, however, was such as to leave a small dent on one who was normally impervious to anything of the sort.

★    ★    ★

While these two small dramas were being enacted, Derek Yates was lying in his prison cell some fifteen miles away. Throughout the night he lay sleepless, his mind feverishly at work.

Less than twenty-four hours later, he had escaped.

## CHAPTER TEN

The news reached Seahaven around five o'clock on a stuffily hot afternoon.

Sergeant Floyd was sitting dourly in his office like a lean brown spider after a particularly satisfying meal. His colleagues in their shirt-sleeves sweated at the sight of him, for he made no concessions to the weather and still wore one of his thick brown suits.

When the telephone rang, his brow crinkled into a slight frown of annoyance as he put out a hand and lifted the receiver. He immediately recognized the voice of Detective Chief Inspector Adams of headquarters.

'Just got word that Yates has escaped', the D.I. said, crisply.

Sergeant Floyd's eyes narrowed.

'How and when?'

'They missed him about an hour ago, but we were only informed a few minutes back; after they'd made a thorough search of the prison and satisfied themselves he really had got away. As to how, that doesn't concern us at the moment.'

'What I meant was, is there any suggestion that he had an accomplice?'

'Not that I've heard.' After a pause Inspector Adams added, 'Anyway, he's scarcely had time to organize that.'

'It could have been fixed in advance.'

Adams appeared to consider this before replying.

'Well, there's no mention of outside help in the message we got. However, I'm going along to see the Governor now, so I'll call you when I know more. The immediate need is to get your chaps on the move as the odds are he'll make for Seahaven. The trouble is there are so many darned hiding-places around there. All those woods and caves on the Rawlins estate...'

'Dogs are the answer. One dog'll be more use than a whole posse of policemen.'

'I'll see what I can arrange, but meanwhile alert everyone.'

With that, the D.I. rang off, leaving Floyd softly cursing prisons which couldn't even hold their inmates for twenty-four hours. He had little doubt that Inspector Adams was right in opining that Yates would head for Seahaven. The question was, what bait would be most likely to lure him into a trap.

He unlocked a drawer in his desk and took out a flat black pistol. He slipped in a clip of ammunition and thoughtfully weighed it in the palm of his hand. Then, with sudden decision, he unloaded it and returned it to the drawer, which he locked.

Though God knows why one shouldn't shoot at the bastard, he thought savagely. It would be the quickest way to teach prisoners to stop where the State put them. Trouble was public opinion—soppy, sentimental, ham-stringing public opinion, which seemed to expect the police to maintain law and order with the aid of biblical texts and fairy wands.

Meanwhile, however, Yates had to be caught before anything worse happened. That something worse could happen, Floyd felt uneasily sure, and this view was shared by others as the news percolated through the town.

★     ★     ★

Indeed, Yates's escape provided one of the main topics of conversation at the reception given that evening by the Mayor of Seahaven in honour of Mr. Justice Dent. Held in the council chamber of the Town Hall, everyone who counted for anything in civic life was present. Jennie, however, had sent her last-minute apologies for 'unavoidable absence'.

The room was unbearably hot, the buzz of conversation deafening and the refreshments of indifferent quality. Added to which there was nowhere to sit down.

Jeremy had with difficulty procured himself a glass of so-called claret cup (it looked like red ink and contained tired bits of fruit which gave the appearance of being uncertain whether to float or sink) and a ham sandwich from which a limp piece of fat protruded. He was just edging his way across the room to an open window when he heard Mr. Justice Dent's voice behind him.

'Come and talk to us, Harper.'

Jeremy did a precarious about-shuffle to find the judge and Sir Geoffrey standing together. His Lordship wore his best party manner but the High Sheriff was making no attempt to hide an expression of bored impatience.

'I was just saying, what's the use of my sending criminals to prison if they're allowed to walk out again after a few hours. I thought that fellow Yates looked a bit of a deep one at times.'

Jeremy shot Sir Geoffrey a quick glance. Either the judge was wholly ignorant of Yates's connection with the Rawlins family or impervious to Sir Geoffrey's susceptibilities. It appeared, however, that the High Sheriff was hardly listening. His eyes were darting about the room and all semblance of polite interest had faded from his expression.

'It was an interesting case', the judge continued expansively. 'It's clear the fellow must have had an accomplice, of course. How else did he dispossess himself of the money?'

Jeremy nodded and took a sip at his claret cup which also *tasted* as much like red ink as anything else. Mr. Justice Dent added coyly:

'I have my own theory about what happened.'

'What is that, Judge?' Jeremy asked, while Sir Geoffrey quickly refocused his attention.

'I haven't any doubt that Yates faked the robbery, mind you, but I don't believe he was working just for himself and a similarly humble accomplice. *I'm* of the opinion that he was used by one of the big gangs—paid in fact to hand over the cash to them and pretend he'd been robbed.' Encouraged by his audience's apparent interest, he continued, 'I think this gang decided it was time they employed a fresh gambit in carrying out one of their robberies and hit upon this idea.'

'I'm afraid it doesn't sound a very likely idea to me', Sir Geoffrey said.

'Not?'

'No. I agree that Yates must have had an accomplice, but I think all this suggestion of gangs and master-crooks is, not to put too fine a point on it, so much piffle. I don't know why anyone wants to look further than the very straightforward facts which were proved in court.' A moment later he murmured an excuse and left the judge and Jeremy.

'Nevertheless, I still stick to my theory', Mr. Justice Dent said good-humouredly and then asked suddenly, 'How did you enjoy the role of a witness?'

'I prefer that of an advocate, Judge.'

'Somewhat different, aren't they? I suspect you found it a chastening experience and I hope you'll remember how you felt next time you're harrying some unfortunate layman who has come to give evidence in one of your cases.'

Jeremy smiled wryly. It occurred to him that this was a prime example of the pot exhorting the kettle not to get black. Soon afterwards, the judge was borne away by the Mayoress and Jeremy took the opportunity of slipping out of the room for a breath of air.

When he returned, he bumped into Sir

Geoffrey who had apparently also just come back in.

'What a bore these functions are', Sir Geoffrey said, looking around him with distaste. 'All they do is give one a filthy headache. I suppose there's no news as to whether they've yet caught Yates?' Jeremy shook his head. 'I shall have to seriously consider asking for police protection so long as he remains at large. Not for myself, of course. For Jennie. If I find him anywhere near my place, I'll break his neck with my own hands.'

With this ominous declaration, he turned and walked off, leaving Jeremy to gaze thoughtfully after him. A few moments later Jeremy moved and leant gratefully against a door post. He reckoned it was almost time when he could decently depart.

The noise and heat inside the room had reached new heights of awfulness. By contrast the rest of the Town Hall was embalmed in a musty, tomblike silence.

And tomblike not only in the metaphorical sense, for since the party had begun, murder had been committed within its walls.

In the Clerk of Assize's office, strangled with a piece of pink tape, Sylvia Ainsworth lay dead.

# CHAPTER ELEVEN

Mr. Swinbank and Waygood both arrived late at the office the next morning.

By sitting till after six o'clock the previous evening, Mr. Justice Dent had managed to complete his last case. So all that remained to be done by the Clerk of Assize and his staff before bidding each other tearless farewells and scattering for the long vacation was half a day's clearing up. Consequently it was around eleven o'clock before either of them put in an appearance. Mr. Swinbank had intended to arrive earlier but the mayoral reception had brought him a restless night and an uneasy morning.

'Sylvia not here?' he asked, as he hung his hat and umbrella on the only available peg.

'Haven't seen her', Waygood replied without bothering to look up from his desk. A peevish frown passed across Mr. Swinbank's brow.

'I wonder what's happened to her.' There was no answer. 'Have you any idea why she's late?'

'Why should I have?'

'I thought perhaps she might have mentioned to you that she was going to be.'

'No, she didn't.'

Waygood's tone was abrupt and his manner

very different from the usual garrulous interference in the lives of others. Even Mr. Swinbank, with his senses dimmed, couldn't fail to observe the change.

'Had a row?' he asked.

'I beg your pardon?' Waygood said frostily.

'You and Sylvia fallen out?' Mr. Swinbank persisted mischievously.

'I'm sure I've no idea what you mean.'

It was a hammy sentence hammily delivered.

'Oh well, I expect she'll turn up soon.' Mr. Swinbank surveyed the tables laden with documents waiting to be packed away. He went on, 'We should be able to get this lot cleared up by early afternoon. When are you off?'

There was no reply and he looked across at Waygood who was drawing deeply on his cigarette and making patently unsuccessful efforts to cast a column of figures.

'I asked you when you're going', Mr. Swinbank repeated.

'Maybe tomorrow: maybe the next day. It all depends', Waygood said in an abstracted tone.

Mr. Swinbank clucked at the information (or lack of it) and said:

'I shan't be here after lunchtime tomorrow, so if there is anything outstanding and you've also gone, Sylvia will have to see to it. However I don't suppose she'll mind looking in as she'll only be at her cottage.'

'What about Yates's escape?' Waygood said

suddenly.

'What about it?' retorted Mr. Swinbank, eyeing his pipe as if it might be a rare archaeological find. Somehow it tasted vile this morning. Another legacy from the mayoral reception, he supposed.

'It's possible the police may wish to see us about it.'

'Whatever for? Anyway, I don't propose to sit about Seahaven on that off-chance.' He looked across at his Clerk of Indictments. 'What's his escape got to do with us?' he asked curiously.

'It occurred to me they might want to look at some of the court documents.'

'Well, they'll have to burrow for them', Mr. Swinbank said, fishing a yellow boiled sweet from the bag in his pocket. He got up and walked over to one of the large wicker hampers. 'Here, give me a hand with this', he puffed, straining to tug it into the middle of the floor.

Instead, however, Waygood flung open the lid; to reveal Sylvia Ainsworth curled embryonically at the bottom.

    ★     ★     ★

Mr. Swinbank and Waygood nervously watched Sergeant Floyd as he bent over the hamper. Straightening himself, he said:

'Nobody's to touch anything. She's obviously

been dead some hours and I want the doctor to see her before she's moved. Photographs will have to be taken too.'

'Poor child! What an end!' Mr. Swinbank exclaimed softly.

'The fiend', Waygood murmured in a voice full of emotion.

Floyd looked quickly from the one to the other.

'Who?'

'The murderer of course', Waygood replied.

'You sounded as though you had a particular person in mind.'

Waygood hesitated.

'Well, haven't we all?' he said. 'Isn't it obviously Yates?'

'What makes you connect Yates's escape with Miss Ainsworth's death?'

Waywood hesitated again and for longer.

'You'll find the two are connected all right', he said at length, with a return of some of his old self-assurance.

'Possibly; but what grounds have you for being so positive about it?'

'I'll tell you later.'

'Too true you will', Floyd replied grimly. 'Seems to me you know quite a bit.'

To anyone who knew Hubert Waygood it was apparent that he was torn between his natural quest for limelight and an inhibiting sense of caution. Moreover, a possible explanation for this had just occurred to Floyd.

There was a brisk knock on the door and Dr. Runce, the Home Office pathologist for the area, came in followed by a police photographer.

Dr. Runce was a person of enormous vitality who always managed to convey an impression of omnipresence. Nobody more than he enjoyed the cut and thrust of forensic contests, and a searching cross-examination (when he knew he was on firm ground) was for him an exquisite pleasure.

'You better take your photographs before I disturb things', he said after a cursory look at Sylvia's crumpled form. While the photographer got to work, Dr. Runce departed into a corner of the room and dictated a preliminary note to his secretary, a placid female who for years past had been his faithful shadow at courts, mortuaries and the scenes of numerous grisly crimes. He completed his dictation and returned to the hamper. 'Finished? Good, then give me a hand to get her out.'

Mr. Swinbank let out a startled exclamation. 'Surely not in here!'

The pathologist looked at him in surprise.

'You don't mind, do you? There won't be any mess.'

Mr. Swinbank shrugged his shoulders in resignation and removed himself to the far end of the room where from time to time he glanced at the proceedings with an expression of mixed repugnance and fascination. Though, as Clerk of Assize, he had sat through countless murder trials and gazed unmoved at numerous albums of gruesome photographs (photographs of far nastier sights than poor Sylvia's dead body) he now felt physically sick. As the body was laid none too gently on the floor, he turned away and tightly closed his eyes.

'Strangled by a piece of office tape', Dr. Runce announced briefly.

'From behind by the look of it', Floyd added, nodding at the knot which showed at the back of the neck. Elsewhere the tape had cut deep into the soft flesh which had almost folded over it.

'Yes, her attacker obviously got behind her and must have applied maximum pressure from the very start. Those scratch marks on her neck clearly indicate where she tried to get her fingers beneath the ligature.'

For some minutes the doctor and police officers busied themselves round the body. Then Sergeant Floyd went over to where Mr. Swinbank was sitting hunched in a corner.

'We shall want to make a thorough search of your office', he said. 'It's possible the murderer has left some clue or other, so perhaps it'd be best if you moved out for the next few hours.'

Mr. Swinbank got up and, after steeling

himself for a final quick look at Sylvia's distorted features, made for the door. Waygood was about to follow him when Floyd put out a hand.

'I'd like to have a few words with you.' As he spoke he motioned him back to where he'd been sitting and turned once more to Dr. Runce, who was engaged in dictating some further notes to his secretary.

'. . . From external examination, death would appear to be due to asphyxia following strangulation by a ligature; the ligature being a piece of pink tape of approximately thirty-six inches in length. Death probably occurred between twelve and eighteen hours ago. That is, between six o'clock and midnight yesterday . . .'

'She was alive at . . . well after six o'clock', Waygood suddenly broke in.

'Very possibly.'

'I mean, I *know* that she was.'

'What time did *you* see her?' Floyd asked sharply.

'About half-past seven.'

'Where?'

'Out at her cottage.'

Floyd nodded.

'You must tell me more about this in a moment', he said in a velvet-glove tone of voice. He turned to the ambulance men who had just arrived and were lifting Sylvia's body on to a stretcher. Dr. Runce also watched them and when they were ready led the way out of the room.

A few timidly curious denizens of the Town Hall stood back as Sylvia made her last journey from the building in which she had worked and died.

'And now we can have our little talk', Floyd said when he and Waygood were alone. Waygood crossed one leg over the other and assumed a self-important air.

'Yes, well, it must have been about half-past seven, I went out to her cottage—nothing unusual about my visit, you understand. I quite often used to go and see her in the evenings—very lonely for her out there, you know—and I found her in a very strange mood. Didn't want me to stay: pretended all sorts of things to try and get rid of me. You know what women can be like sometimes. So after a bit I left and drove back into town. It must have been around a quarter past eight, I suppose.' There was a short silence and Waygood went on, 'Of course it's quite obvious now why she acted so strangely. Either Yates was hiding in the cottage or she was expecting him.'

'What makes you so sure of that?'

'It's the only explanation of recent events. You can take it from me, Sergeant, Sylvia hadn't been herself these past few weeks. Looking back now, I can see that she first started behaving oddly about the time of the

Yates robbery. Since then there've been little things I've noticed from time to time. Added together, I'm certain there was some tie-up between Yates and herself.' He nimbly recrossed his legs the other way and continued, 'In any event it's far too much of a coincidence that Yates escapes from prison one day and she's murdered the next. It's obvious the two events are related.'

'What *sort* of small things did you notice about her which make you say there must have been a link between them?'

Waygood cocked his head and assumed a gravely portentous air.

'Well, now, let me think', he said slowly. 'There were so many, it's difficult to know which to mention. I mean by themselves they probably don't amount to much. It's the total impression they made on me that I'm going on.' There ensued a silence in which he was conscious of Sergeant Floyd's steady gaze. At length he said, 'For example, she behaved very queerly during Yates's trial. Avoided coming into court...'

'I saw her there quite a bit.'

'Y-yes, she came in from time to time, but ... You see that's just what I mean; as soon as one starts trying to pinpoint individual incidents it's hopeless.' Huffily he added, 'Anyway, I personally haven't any doubt that she and Yates were up to something and that it's he who has murdered her.'

'It sounds to me very much like a case of the wish being father to the thought.'

'You can scoff if you want, but I bet I'll turn out to be right.'

'Let's try another line', Floyd said. 'Do I gather that the last you saw of Miss Ainsworth was about a quarter past eight yesterday evening out at her cottage?'

'Yes, about then. I can't swear to the exact minute.'

'It'd be suspicious if you could', Floyd observed dryly. 'You're sure about that? The time and place, I mean?'

'Certainly I am.'

'Did she tell you she proposed returning to the office later?'

'No.'

'Any reason you know of why she should have come back here?'

'None. She quite often used to, after supper, when there was a rush on, but there was certainly no occasion for her to do so last night. Everything was almost cleared up.'

'How do you think she got down here?'

'I haven't a clue. She might have cycled—that was what she normally did. She might even have walked.'

'Or got a lift?'

Waygood shrugged his shoulders.

'I suppose so', he said.

106

'But you wouldn't know?' Floyd pressed.

'No idea, Sergeant.' It was at this point he appeared to notice that Floyd was writing something. He nodded towards his open notebook. 'What are you writing down?' he asked in a suspicious tone.

'Just a few notes of our conversation. Nothing to get worried about.'

But for some reason it seemed that Waygood was worried and for the remainder of the interview he kept his eyes firmly glued on Sergeant Floyd's pencil.

Floyd went on:

'What did she say to you when you called on her yesterday evening? After all, there must have been some exchange of words between you?'

'I couldn't really get anything coherent out of her. She seemed all jumpy and on edge.'

'But what about?'

'I'll tell you what I think', Waygood said, dropping his voice to a confidential whisper and beginning to slice the air with his right hand to add emphasis to his words. 'I believe there was someone else in all this besides her and Yates.'

'In all what?'

'In whatever it was.'

'Don't be so darned mysterious', Floyd said with exasperation. 'And anyway why do you think there was another person involved with them?'

'Because she made one very cryptic remark just before I left last night. I was trying to find out why she was het-up and at one point she muttered something about a well-known local character being a crook.'

'And that was all?'

'Yes, but it's significant, don't you think? Your guess is as good as mine, but it can't refer to many people.'

'You think you know whom she meant?'

'I'm keeping my thoughts to myself for the time being', Waygood said loftily.

'Right. We'll just get all this down in the form of a written statement', Floyd said, in a purposeful tone.

Waygood started to demur and plead inconvenience, but to no avail.

When at last his evidence had been laboriously recorded and read back to him, he signed it, after first initialling with relish a number of minor corrections he had made to Sergeant Floyd's spelling and punctuation.

'Now I'll take a look around here', Floyd said as he pocketed the statement. He got up and went over to the hamper which lay open and empty in the middle of the floor. It appeared to bring him no inspiration and he went down on hands and knees to peer under the desks. As he crawled slowly around, Waygood watched him in silence. Suddenly Floyd stretched out a hand beneath Sylvia's desk and picked up something.

It was a button.

'Here, let's have a look at that a moment', Waygood said.

Sergeant Floyd's answer was to close his fingers over it and then flash his hand open under Waygood's nose.

'Recognize it?'

'Not one of mine.'

'I didn't imagine it was.'

'Why should I have recognized it then?'

'You might have done.'

Leaving Waygood to worry this out for himself, Floyd continued his search. Apparently satisfied that the room held nothing further of interest, he said:

'I'm going to lock your office now, so you'll have to shift yourself.'

'Where are you going?'

'Out to Miss Ainsworth's cottage.'

'I'll come with you and give you a hand, if you like.'

'I don't', Floyd said, tersely.

'As you wish. But let me know if there's anything further you want from me and I'll also keep you in touch.'

Floyd looked at him warily.

'Don't you start any private eye stuff or you'll be heading for trouble.'

But Waygood merely gave a superior chuckle and walked out of the room.

A few moments later Floyd was on his way

back to the C.I.D. office, having first called in to give a short report on events to the uniformed Chief Inspector who was the head of the Seahaven division of the County Constabulary.

As he climbed the stairs to his own office, he congratulated himself on having got Waywood's signature to a written statement. With grim pleasure he looked forward to the moment when he would confront him with his lies—for lies the statement most certainly contained: provable lies at that.

## CHAPTER TWELVE

At about the time that Sylvia was on her last journey from the Town Hall, Jennie was approaching the top of Piglet Ridge. This feature which was the shape of a pig's back was situated on the Rawlins estate about two miles from the house and was covered, except along its actual top, by a beech wood.

Jennie clambered up the shortest but hardest way and by the time she broke cover at the top, she was hot and dishevelled. Several times she had slipped and fallen on the hard, smooth turf or had had to clutch wildly at the nearest bit of tree when her feet had slithered away in a cascade of small lumps of chalk. For Piglet

Ridge was a hump of solid chalk.

She paused in the shadow of a young tree and leaned gratefully against its trunk. Looking about her, she whistled for Sambo whom she could hear rootling to her left. A moment later he emerged from the wood fifty yards from her and stood waiting for further directions.

'Here, Sambo, here', she called in the clipped, breathy tones usually reserved for conversation with dogs.

He turned instantly and came running to her and sank down at her feet in a state of panting exhaustion. His pink tongue dripped from his mouth, his glossy carcass heaved, but his adoring eyes never left her face. She bent and tickled him behind an ear and for a brief moment he ceased panting to acknowledge the gesture.

'You're more out of breath than I am', she said to him, 'but then you've been four times as far to get here. And what have you picked up in the way of scents? Nothing; absolutely nothing—except a few for your own amusement. And that's not the reason I've brought you out here.' She gave him a final pat and said, 'Now you've got to do better.' As she spoke, she pulled a man's sock from her pocket and held it over the dog's nose. He turned his head as if to indicate he was not in the mood for woolly socks but Jennie persisted. 'Now for the caves', she said, straightening up.

111

On the far side of the ridge, there were three caves. One large and two much smaller ones. They looked out over the fields to the distant cliffs which sheltered Seahaven from the prevailing winds. As Jennie clambered over the top of Piglet Ridge and dropped down the other side, she felt her heart-beats quicken and a sickness in her stomach.

A few yards farther on, she halted. She was now able to see the caves; or rather the place where she knew them to be, for nature had provided perfect camouflage.

There was no sign of life, either present or recent. She tried to induce Sambo to reconnoitre the caves, but he merely weaved about aimlessly without going anywhere near the entrances. When her eyes and ears ached with the strain of concentrated watching and listening, she moved cautiously forward.

She had been so certain that something would have happened by now. Not for any founded reason but because she had had a hunch it would. And more often than not her hunches didn't let her down.

About six feet from the entrance to the largest cave, she halted and once more listened intently.

'Here, Sambo', she hissed, waving a hand in the cave's direction. He went up to it but appeared to find nothing to interest him and after a brief pause to pay his respects to a tree returned to her side.

With sudden resolution Jennie walked straight up to the cave entrance and went in. She stopped just inside and, holding her breath in an endeavour to control her thumping heart, looked all around her. There was no more sign of life than there had been outside. Indeed it seemed to her that no one had been there since she and Jeremy and other children had used Piglet Ridge for the most wonderful games.

She suddenly found herself filled with strangely mixed feelings: of relief and anxiety: of tension and general letdown. But before she had time to pursue her thoughts, there was wild barking outside and she shrank back against the cave wall seized with clammy fear.

The barking got nearer and then a human shadow fell across the cave mouth. Jennie felt the panic of a person trapped by the unknown and tried to scream.

'Are you in there, Jennie?'

The voice that asked the question was soft and different and for a second she stood silently in the shadows. She was puzzled.

'Is that you, Jeremy?' she called out nervously.

The shadow moved and there was Jeremy silhouetted in the mouth of the cave.

'What on earth are *you* doing here?' Her tone clearly indicated that alarm had given way to annoyance.

'I might ask you the same question.'

By this time she had joined him outside and Sambo, simple dog that he was, was dancing happily around them.

'It happens to be part of my home and I was having a walk', she said icily.

'I'm sorry if I scared you. But I wasn't sure it was you inside there.'

'Whom did you expect to find?'

'I *hoped* it would be you.'

'But what are you doing on Piglet Ridge at all?'

'Looking for you. I guessed you might be around here.' There was a silence and then he said gently, 'Any sign of him?' Jennie didn't answer but turned away and Jeremy went on, 'Jennie, please listen to a word of warning...?'

'No', she broke in and swung round to face him. 'I don't want any of your homilies so ...' Her tone softened and she gave him a rueful smile. 'Coming back?'

He sighed and fell into step beside her. For some way they walked in uneasy silence.

'Is your father home today?' he asked after a while.

'He's motored up to London, but he's coming back this evening. Quite unnecessarily.'

'How do you mean?'

'He'd normally have stopped the night there as he has more meetings tomorrow, but he refuses to leave me in the house alone.' She tossed her head petulantly. 'Which is ridiculous. And anyway I shouldn't be alone. There are still five servants sleeping in the place.'

'Couldn't you have gone with him?'

'He suggested I should, but I didn't want to.'

'Maybe it would've been a good idea.'

'I'm not interested in what you think are good ideas.'

'Look, Jennie, please listen to me for one little moment.'

'Not if you're only going to run down Derek.'

'But, Jennie . . .' Jeremy's voice trailed away into a hopeless silence. How could he say what he wanted to without sounding insufferably priggish? Yates was an escaped convict with society's hand against him and yet to try and make Jennie see sense was like trying to befriend a porcupine. It almost seemed, however, that she read his thoughts for she said suddenly and with an air of finality:

'As far as I'm concerned, Derek's innocent. The jury were taken in by a lot of false evidence.'

'You can't really believe that, Jennie. Good God, next you'll be telling me I committed perjury.'

'You know better than I whether that cap fits', she replied tartly. Then rubbing further salt into his wounds, she added, 'After all, it was largely on your cleverly slanted evidence that he was convicted.'

When Jeremy was hurt, as now, his expression invariably became stuffy as a bishop's at a convention of hedonists. Though he and Jennie continued to walk side by side, they did so in a stony silence. So far as Jeremy was concerned, he'd done his best; but if, as seemed to be the case, Jennie was determined to play with fire, she must burn her fingers and learn the hard way. And moreover, thought Jeremy, if she burns them worse than seems likely, as may well happen, she'll still have only herself to blame.

Since leaving Piglet Ridge, they had been plunging through woods and over fields in the general direction of the house. As they approached Sylvia's cottage, Jennie, who was a pace or so in front, suddenly halted.

'Look, there's Daddy's car', she said in a startled voice, nodding in the direction of the drive where Sir Geoffrey's dove-grey Rolls-Bentley shone resplendently. In her surprise, their recent quarrel was forgotten.

'So I see', Jeremy replied stiffly, determined not to lay himself open to further reproof.

'But what's it doing there?'

Even as she spoke, Sir Geoffrey appeared round the side of the cottage, gave it a quick last look and got into his car, driving off a moment later in the direction of the Hall.

Jennie looked anxiously at Jeremy whose expression was completely impassive.

'This is where our ways part', he said and turning his back on her, stalked off.

Jennie hurried back to the house to find her father pacing up and down the drawing-room.

'Ah! there you are', he said as soon as she opened the door.

'What's happened, Daddy? Why haven't you gone up to London?'

'You won't have heard, of course', he said in a faintly pompous tone. 'When I called at the mill on my way, I learnt that Sylvia had been found murdered.'

'Oh, no!' The words came out in stunned incredulity.

'I'm afraid so. Her body was found this morning in the Clerk of Assize's office.' For a few moments he left his daughter to ponder the implications. Then breaking the silence he went on, 'I've been over to Franwich and had a word with the Chief Constable. I've persuaded him to call in Scotland Yard.'

★ ★ ★

It was lunchtime before Sergeant Floyd arrived at the cottage. He parked his car out of sight of the road and approached the front door, almost with the air of a mortal stumbling on a gingerbread house in the depths of the magic forest. He had taken the key from Sylvia's handbag and now let himself in, softly closing the door behind him.

A search is inevitably more difficult when one has no idea what one is looking for, and for a while Floyd just stood in the small parlour peering about him intently and absorbing every detail. Once or twice he put out a hand to pick up some object or other which he proceeded to examine with thoughtful care. He gave particular attention to some letters and odd pieces of paper lying on the small side table which Sylvia had used as a writing-desk. None of them appeared to have any significance.

He moved into the small neat kitchen. There, nothing was out of place apart from two upturned cups and saucers on the draining board, which had obviously been washed and left to dry. Next he climbed the narrow staircase to the tiny landing off which the two bedrooms led. One was not much larger than a cupboard and didn't appear to have been in recent use. The other was Sylvia's room. Floyd went in. With an air of feline detachment, he opened a drawer here and there and burrowed daintily amongst the contents. Suddenly it came to him that something was missing: something that the cottage lacked but which for the moment he couldn't call to mind. It was only when he was contemplating the glass menagerie on the mantel piece that it dawned on him what was wrong. It was a complete absence of photographs in any of the rooms.

Rare indeed is the home where no one gazes out on the scene from between the walls of a picture frame. It may be Mum and Dad starry-eyed on their wedding day or brother Syd looking sheepish in uniform, but there's almost sure to be someone propped up over the fireplace or on a bedside table.

The more he thought about this, the more Floyd realized that there was something impersonal about Sylvia's home. Nowhere did it provide any clue to the sort of person who had lived in it. All that could be learnt was that its occupant had gone out expecting to return and then hadn't done so, which, he reflected grimly, was almost certainly the precise way it had been.

He returned to the ground floor and pulled open a cupboard-like door beneath the stairs to reveal a sharp flight of stone steps leading down into Stygian blackness. He ran his hand up and down the wall just inside the door till he felt the light switch, which he turned on.

The steps were smooth and in places dangerously worn so that he descended with caution. Over in one corner of the cellar was an old stove which had at one time been used for heating the water. Floyd walked straight over to it and started fishing around the interior with a long iron rod. A moment later he extracted a piece of coarse, grey cloth.

He repeated the operation and by the time he had finished had removed further pieces, most of them bearing signs of having been burnt. He examined them. It was apparent that one of the pieces came from the front of some sort of jacket. It had a line of cheap buttons which had proved incombustible, and he noticed that one was missing.

The cloth was prison grey and the buttons identical with the one which he had found in the Clerk of Assize's office.

*     *     *

It was about half past two when Floyd got back to the C.I.D. office feeling rather pleased with himself.

'Inspector Adams has been on the phone for you, Sarge', said Detective-Constable Ingram by way of greeting.

'Anything special?'

'He wants you to call him back as soon as possible.'

'Did he say whether he was coming over this afternoon?'

'No.'

'I expect he will; though there's nothing we can't manage provided headquarters give us a bit of extra help.' Ingram nodded keenly. 'Did he say anything further about Yates's escape?'

'No, Sarge.'

'I'd better call him and find out what he wants.' He turned to go but paused. 'Everything else under control? Grant's still at the p.m. I suppose, and I take it Shepherd and Myers are out on the inquiries I sent them to make?'

Ingram nodded, and satisfied that his team were all at work Floyd disappeared into his office to phone headquarters.

'Sergeant Floyd here, Inspector. I understand you've been trying to get me.' Although the two men had known one another for over twenty years, Floyd's formality on the telephone had never grown less.

'Yes, I wanted to tell you that the Chief has requested the Yard's assistance in the Ainsworth case. I gather Detective-Superintendent Manton is likely to be coming down.'

'But why?' Floyd asked with an edge to his tone. 'We've hardly had a chance to get anywhere yet. The body was only discovered a few hours ago, but there's no reason for thinking we can't handle the case ourselves. What's he want to call in the Yard for? What's . . . ?'

'Look, Sergeant, that's what he has done, so there's no point in all these questions.'

'Well, he hasn't lost any time over it', Floyd observed sourly. 'He can't have much

121

confidence in his own force if he's not even willing to give them a chance of solving a straightforward murder case.'

Detective-Inspector Adams sighed. Not that he had expected Floyd to react any differently and he knew there was no point in trying to win him over. Added to which he himself was a trifle irked at the alacrity the Chief Constable had shown in the matter. Admittedly not many murders were committed in the county and this was the first for four years that looked like being a proper one. (In the eyes of the police, a 'proper' murder was one in which there was no doubt that the victim had been *murdered*, the only issue being whether the evidence was sufficient to convict the accused. Mad murders, sad murders, and murders which were really manslaughters were heaped together and regarded somewhat differently.) But there was still no reason why the County C.I.D. shouldn't have been given a chance to get on with the case. He, Inspector Adams, felt completely confident of their capacity to do a thorough job and it was clear that Sergeant Floyd had no doubts on that score either.

Floyd was speaking again.

'So you know what made him?'

'It was after he'd had a chat with Sir Geoffrey Rawlins.'

'That explains a lot of things.'

'Such as?' Adams asked, and then wished he

hadn't. But there was no need for him to have worried.

'Confirms a hunch I've had since the supposed robbery', Floyd replied. 'I won't talk about it now.'

'O.K., Sergeant. I'll leave you to press on with your inquiries. If Superintendent Manton comes down from London this afternoon, I'll wait and bring him over. Otherwise I'll be along myself within the next couple of hours.'

'I see', Floyd said flatly and replaced the receiver. For some time afterwards he sat staring out of the window. What the Chief had done, he'd done. But Floyd didn't like it. And he liked it still less as he brooded on it.

There was a tap on the door and in a moment Floyd was alert.

'Come in.'

It was Detective-Constable Grant.

'I've just come back from the mortuary, Sergeant.'

'Runce finished his p.m.?'

'Yes. Straightforward job. Asphyxia due to strangulation by a ligature', Grant said with the youthfully blasé air of one who had been attending his second post-mortem examination.

'What else?'

'How do you mean, Sergeant?'

'Any defence injuries? Any bruises indicating a struggle? All you've told me is the cause of death and I knew that already.'

'No, not a thing. There wasn't a mark on her body apart from the neck. Dr. Runce says there can't have been any struggle and she died in a matter of seconds.'

'But I thought there were some scratch marks on the neck. In fact I know there were because I saw them. What did he have to say about those?'

Grant looked nonplussed. He knew that Floyd had a passion for detail but he would have to await the pathologist's full report if he wanted a description of the body pore by pore.

'He just said they'd been caused by her trying to get her fingers beneath the ligature to save herself.'

'Well, that's very important.'

'But you already knew it, Sergeant.'

'Maybe I did; but you didn't know that I knew till I mentioned it just now. An eye for detail, Grant, that's what makes a good detective.' Detective-Constable Grant stared stonily at his sergeant but refrained from comment. Floyd went on, 'Anyway was there anything at all about the body which might give us a clue to the murderer?'

'Nothing', Grant said, shaking his head vigorously.

Floyd gave a small curt nod.

'O.K.', he said. 'We at least know where we are. I think you and I will now go to Yates's lodgings and see what we can find there.'

*       *       *

As a result of the Chief Constable's telephone conversation with the Assistant Commissioner (Crime) of the Metropolitan Police at Scotland Yard, Detective-Superintendent Simon Manton found himself dispatched to Franwich without even time to pack a toothbrush.

'The sooner you go the better', the A.C.C. had said. 'The Chief Constable has got the wind up. I gather the High Sheriff—a man named Rawlins; I expect you've heard of him: big industrialist and was an M.P.; pots of money—has been on his tail and dropped dark hints about getting in touch direct with his friend the Minister if there aren't some pretty immediate results. And by that he means Yates's recapture. So you cut along now and I'll send you down a sergeant tomorrow.'

Manton was one of the youngest detective-superintendents in the Yard's so-called murder squad. Because he was not only an efficient officer but also one with a high degree of adaptability, he was frequently assigned to cases which required tactful handling in addition to other qualities.

Within half an hour of arriving at county police headquarters at Franwich, he and Detective Chief Inspector Adams were in a car on their way to Seahaven.

125

'What's your set-up there?' Manton asked as the car sped through the outskirts of Franwich and took the left fork which was signposted SEAHAVEN 14³/₄ MILES. The road ran down the wide, fertile valley on the opposite side of the river to the branch railway line which connected the two towns. Soon after leaving Franwich it was possible to get a first salty tang of the sea.

'The C.I.D. consists of a sergeant and four detective-constables. Floyd's the sergeant. Good officer but a prickly customer. Gives the impression of being a bit embittered with life. He wasn't too pleased when he heard the Chief had enlisted the Yard's aid.'

Manton smiled faintly.

'Not an unusual, or unnatural, reaction.'

For the rest of the journey he sat back in silence listening to Inspector Adams's account of the Yates affair (as it had come to be called) and the discovery of Sylvia Ainsworth's dead body.

As they were approaching Seahaven, Adams gave the driver instructions to turn off the main road into a tree-shaded lane which ran up a gently-rising slope. About five minutes later, nodding at the only building in sight, he said:

'That's Sylvia Ainsworth's cottage. And this is the main entrance to Sir Geoffrey's place, though you can't see the Hall from here.'

'Quite a lonely spot', Manton observed, carefully taking in the scene.

Twenty minutes later he and Floyd were shaking hands and making a first covert appraisal of each other.


## CHAPTER THIRTEEN

'Anything fresh since I spoke to you on the phone?' Adams asked when they were all seated in the office of the uniformed Chief Inspector who was in charge of the Seahaven division of the County police.

Sergeant Floyd spoke up, first reporting the autopsy findings; then his search of Sylvia's cottage. He concluded:

'I've been to Yates's lodgings this afternoon, but I found nothing there to help us.'

'Presumably he hasn't been near the place since his arrest four weeks ago.'

'Yeah, and all his belongings have been packed up. They're in a trunk out in the garage. The old lady who owns the house can't say a good word for him now and I'm certain she'd shout for the nearest policeman if she so much as caught a glimpse of him.'

'Was this the first time anyone's been there since his arrest?' Manton asked.

'I'll say not', Floyd replied. 'We gave the whole house a thorough going over when we arrested him. There was always an outside chance that we'd find some clue to the missing cash.'

Manton nodded and Inspector Adams said: 'Who packed his things? The landlady?'

'No, Miss Rawlins. It seems she went there about a week after his arrest and spent an afternoon at it. Said he'd asked her to.'

'Wonder she didn't remove them altogether', Adams said.

'She was probably afraid her father would find out and blow up.'

There was a moment's ruminative silence and then Adams said:

'Anyway it's unlikely Yates would show his face in the town itself. Far too risky.'

Several pairs of interested eyes turned on him. It was the uniformed Chief Inspector who spoke.

'But what about the murder? Aren't you forgetting Miss Ainsworth was killed in the Town Hall?'

'That was under cover of darkness. What I really meant was that he wouldn't dare appear round any of his known haunts.'

Manton said nothing but silently wondered why Yates should keep away from these when he'd apparently had the nerve to enter the Town Hall which, amongst other things, housed the police themselves. Adams went on:

'As you know the search for Yates is being intensified and every inch of ground between here and Franwich is being combed. There's little doubt he's somewhere in the vicinity and on the instructions of the Chief Constable particular attention is to be given to Sir Geoffrey Rawlins' estate. It has more hiding-places than a honeycomb has cells, but with dogs we ought with luck to pick up his scent. In the meantime, all we can do about the murder is to collect all the facts and complete our file of witnesses' statements so that when we do nab sonny, we'll know exactly what to throw at him.' He looked across to Manton and said, 'I think Mr. Manton agrees with that, as we discussed it with the Chief and in the car coming over.'

Manton nodded and said:

'The only real piece of evidence at the moment to connect Yates with the murder, as I understand it, is the button which was found near the body and which appears to have come from the half-burnt prison jacket which Sergeant Floyd found at the cottage. The one proves—or purports to prove—a link between her and Yates. The other is, of course, evidence pointing to Yates as the murderer.' He spoke in a slightly detached manner as though trying out his theories on himself.

'Unless . . .' It was Sergeant Floyd who, looking straight towards him, claimed attention and went on, 'Unless both the button and the prison clothes are deliberate plants by someone out to incriminate Yates. Is that perhaps what's in your mind?'

Manton was momentarily taken aback at being so suddenly confronted by what was no more than a half-formed thought at the back of his mind. Shrugging off the question he said:

'I suppose that's just a possibility; but don't let's discard the obvious until it's been proved false. And at the moment what is obvious is that Yates murdered Miss Ainsworth.'

The silence that followed was broken by Floyd. Speaking with quiet emphasis, he said:

'There's someone who is very intent on getting Yates out of the way—for good.'

'Who?' asked Inspector Adams.

'I don't know. I can only guess, and I'm no better at that than you. But of this I am certain. Once we can get at the real truth of the Yates robbery affair and find out who was behind it, the rest will be simple.' As an afterthought, he added with a mirthless smile, 'Perhaps I sound as though I'm holding a brief for Yates. In which case just you wait till he's found.'

'Who was the last person to see Miss Ainsworth alive?' Manton asked, after Floyd's remarks had been suitably pondered.

'Hubert Waygood.' Floyd opened the folder on his lap and produced Waygood's signed statement. He read out the last two paragraphs.

'Not terribly helpful', Manton observed. 'We still don't know what caused her to return to the

Town Hall or how she got there.'

'We know the latter', Floyd said. 'She came by car.' All attention was immediately focused on him. 'It so happens I was on my way home off duty when I saw her get out of a car on the opposite side of the square to the Town Hall.'

'What time was this?' Manton asked.

'It must have been a few minutes before half past eight.'

'Couldn't you see whose car it was?' Adams asked sharply.

'Most certainly. That's what makes this statement more interesting than it seems. It was Waygood's car and Waygood was driving it.'

★       ★       ★

When the conference was ready to break up, the uniformed Chief Inspector suddenly said:

'It's a bit late to say so, Mr. Manton, but we're glad to welcome you and anything we can do to help is yours for the asking. I speak, of course, for all the officers of my division who've been told to co-operate with you to the fullest extent.'

'Thank you, Chief Inspector', Manton replied gravely. 'I'm sure I shall both need and get their co-operation.'

'What do you want to do first?' asked Inspector Adams.

'I'd like to spend a quiet half-hour reading

your file on the robbery job.'

'And after that?'

'Go along to the paper mill and nose about there a bit.'

Sergeant Floyd's eyes glinted.

'You agree then that's where the whole case begins?' he said.

'That's one of the things I hope to find out.'


# CHAPTER FOURTEEN

For Jeremy the long vacation was not going at all as planned.

He had been looking forward to a quiet week at home, followed by a three weeks visit to the Costa Brava with two friends and an ancient motor-car. He had promised William, the clerk to his chambers, that he would stay in Seahaven for the remainder of the vacation and be on call for any work that might come in.

William never tired of rubbing into the younger members of chambers that August was *their* month—the month when the great ones deserted the Temple in search of much-needed rest, leaving the field open to them.

'You stick around in August, Mr. Harper and, who knows, by October you'll have earned yourself a reputation', William had said to Jeremy one day at the end of the Summer term when holidays were under discussion. It was his regular exhortation to his young men and though sincerely given was always received with a considerable degree of scepticism.

Jeremy's memory of last year's long Summer vacation was of spending the whole of it at home on William's advice, waiting for telephone calls to bring him news of fat briefs requiring instant attention. In the event there had been but one phone call followed the next day by an extremely slender brief requiring him to appear for an even slenderer fee at a Magistrates' Court some sixty miles away. Decked out in black jacket and striped trousers, he had arrived there to learn that the case had been adjourned owing to his client's near-successful attempt to gas himself that morning. He had left the court and taken a melancholy stroll along the crowded promenade where his appearance had aroused interest, if not ribald comment, among the town's visitors. It was a large and popular holiday resort and Jeremy could not have felt more out of place if he'd been dressed as an Old Testament prophet.

All this had passed through his mind when William had earnestly repeated the advice again this year. Reputation for what? he had wanted to ask caustically, but had not.

On learning of the projected trip to Spain,

William had clucked solemnly and said with a sigh:

'I suppose if you must, Mr. Harper. I only hope your practice won't suffer too much though. August is the season of ripe plums, don't forget.' He had smacked his lips and left Jeremy to picture all the thousand-guinea briefs which would have to be turned away because of his absence. In the end Jeremy had agreed to cut his trip by a week.

'Don't know why everyone nowadays wants to rush off to these foreign places', William had persisted after the compromise had been reached. 'Particularly when you live in a nice town like Seahaven. And I'm told Spain is very backward and that it's wholly unsafe to drink the water.'

'Who wants to, anyway?' one of Jeremy's stable companions had cheerfully asked. 'It's the food, the sun and the girls that count. In the reverse order, *of course.*' At this point William had retired.

And now here was Jeremy at home and as far removed from a holiday spirit as a polar bear from the Equator. In the light of recent events he had cancelled all idea of going to Spain and told his friends they must leave without him. He had, however, refrained from notifying William of his change of plan. It was preferable that the clerk should believe him to be out of reach for the next week or so.

On the morning after Superintendent Manton's arrival in Seahaven, Jeremy was walking aimlessly along the road which led out of the town past Sir Geoffrey's paper mill in the direction of the river estuary. He was mentally kicking a pebble before him and never heard the car come up behind. Indeed the first thing he was aware of was a voice saying, 'Step in if you're not going anywhere particular.'

He turned to find the door of the pale grey Rolls-Bentley open and Sir Geoffrey leaning across towards him from the driving seat. There was no one else in the car; not even Mason the chauffeur who was normally as much of a fixture as the steering-wheel.

A trifle nonplussed, Jeremy got in and slammed the door.

'Out for a stroll?' Sir Geoffrey asked as he pulled the car away from the kerb.

'Yes, sir', Jeremy replied.

There was an awkward silence, then Sir Geoffrey said:

'Still no sign of that blackguard, Yates. They say they've searched the whole of my estate and not found a trace of him. If you ask me, they're relying too much on dogs and not enough on human observation. Dogs may be all very fine for some types of police work, but they're not a substitute for brains and intelligence.'

From this, Jeremy formed a picture of one stolid constable and a pack of hounds trapesing fruitlessly over Sir Geoffrey's acres.

'Have they now finished their search?' he asked.

'Good lord, no. There are still some officers scouting around.'

'They seem pretty certain that Yates is hiding somewhere on your property, sir.'

'Yes, everyone appears to think it's the most likely place to find him', Sir Geoffrey agreed grimly and added, 'there is, after all, one very good reason for him to come sniffing back there.' Jeremy waited and the other said, 'The money, of course.'

'The money?'

'Well, isn't it what you'd expect him to do in the circumstances. Creep back to the spot where he's hidden the spoil and then get out for good in double-quick time? Right out— Tangier, South America: the farther the better.'

'I see', Jeremy said slowly, after pondering awhile. 'I hadn't realized where . . . that . . . that the money was . . .'

'Hidden somewhere on the estate? You hadn't thought of that?'

'No, it hadn't occurred to me', he replied and went on, 'I mean, are there any grounds for thinking so?'

At that moment, Sir Geoffrey swung the car hard over to the right. It swooshed through the main entrance to the mill as he accelerated with what Jeremy felt was a seigniorial disregard for the few stray employees who were about. He pulled up in the special parking place reserved for him and abruptly remarked:

'The police have been nosing around here, too. Damn nuisance they can be. And I specially asked the Chief Constable to ensure they got in touch with me first.'

Although Jeremy had no particular mission that morning and might therefore as well be sitting in a car park as doing anything else, he could not help feeling a trifle awkward.

He wondered whether he should now take the initiative in alighting and thanking Sir Geoffrey for a lift he hadn't wanted or whether he ought to wait for the great man to make the first move.

'At least you and I are agreed on one thing, I hope', Sir Geoffrey said, while Jeremy was still deciding which course to adopt. 'Namely that Yates was properly convicted.' As he spoke he wound up the driver's window.

'The jury didn't seem to have any doubts', Jeremy replied with a touch of forced heartiness.

'And you?'

'As a lawyer, I . . .'

'No, as an ordinary person', Sir Geoffrey broke in.

'It seemed a clear enough case against him.'

'It did, didn't it?' Leaving the subject on this enigmatic note, he suddenly said, 'How about your coming to spend a few days at the Hall? It'd be nice for Jennie to have your company.' He noticed the look of doubt that passed across Jeremy's face. 'And I should be more than glad to know you were there keeping an eye on her. Too busy myself to stop at home every day. But I don't want to return one evening and find my daughter's flown. So you'll come, won't you? Just pack a bag and go along there this afternoon. I'll phone and tell Mrs. Drake to get a room ready for you.'

'But surely you're not expecting Jennie to . . . to . . .'

'Disappear to Tangier or South America?' Sir Geoffrey's tone was grimly sardonic. He put in his monocle and turning the full force of his gaze on to Jeremy said, 'Good! You'll come then.'

★   ★   ★

After leaving Sir Geoffrey, Jeremy continued his walk. The dunes that clustered at the river mouth were deserted and provided him with the solitude he felt he needed. For more than two hours he wandered through them deep in faraway thought until he was well up the coast. Then, cutting inland, he quickened his pace to arrive home just as his mother was laying the table for lunch.

Without ado, he told her of his new plans.

'That'll be nice for you, dear', she said cosily. 'I've been wondering about you and Jennie recently.' Mrs. Harper knew enough not to expect her son to encourage her views on this subject. Undismayed by his stony look she went on, 'Wondering whether now everything's over between her and that dreadful young man, you mightn't become friends again.'

'We've never ceased being friends', Jeremy said stiffly.

'Oh, you know what I mean, dear', she said with a sigh. 'Jennie'd make such a nice wife.'

It was Jeremy's turn to sigh.

'I dare say she would; but I'm hardly in a position to support such a luxury.'

'You don't want to leave these things too late, dear.'

'But dammit, Mother, I'm only twenty-five.'

'Twenty-six next birthday', Mrs. Harper replied, unanswerably.

The truth was that, more than anything, she longed to be a grandmother. Jeremy was her only child and she was obsessed by the ridiculous thought of the two of them growing older and older till all hope was gone and she was left with a middle-aged bachelor son whose balding head and bulging waistline spelt ruin to romance. It was an unlikely and quite unnecessarily dreary picture. It accounted, however, for the quiet pleasure with which she received his news of moving up to the Hall for a few days.

Reclaiming her mind from the gloomy tracks along which it had been running, she brightened and said:

'Anyway, I'm so glad, as it'll help to make up for the disappointment of not going to Spain with Roger and Ethel.'

'Roger and *Tim*', Jeremy said. 'I thought you told me one of your friends was called Ethel.'

'Ethel's the name of the car, Mother.' As an afterthought, he added. 'I'm happy to say I don't know anyone of that awful name.'

'There was a cousin of your father's who lived at Herne Bay—or do I mean Herne Hill? No, I know, it was Hadley Wood. Her name was Ethel. I took you to see her once when you were a little boy. I don't suppose you remember.'

'No', said Jeremy firmly and made to go and prepare himself for lunch.

'It'll also mean I can get on and distemper the kitchen', Mrs. Harper continued, determined to wring every drop of good from the situation. 'I've got all the stuff and had intended doing it while you were abroad. Now I can start this afternoon. I think it'll look very nice when it's finished. The colour is called "Cloud of Glory" and it looks like lemon curd.'

Jeremy fled. After lunch, in which he studiously kept the conversation off his own

140

affairs, he retired to his room to pack and Mrs. Harper went to hers to contemplate the new kitchen colour scheme.

Shortly before five o'clock, he set out for the Hall in his mother's car. It was arranged that either he or one of Sir Geoffrey's staff would bring it back that evening in time for her to go to a canasta party.

As he drove out of Seahaven, he noticed figures moving on the skyline to his left. He could see that they were in uniform and wore flat peaked caps. A little farther along the road, a police officer stepped suddenly out of the hedgerow and signalled him to stop. Jeremy did so and the officer, a motor patrol one from county police headquarters, came up to the car.

'Excuse me, sir, you got any passengers with you?' he asked, peering round the car's interior.

'As you can see, none.'

'Haven't seen anyone trying to thumb a lift, I suppose?'

'No.'

'Mind if I look in the boot, sir?'

'Go ahead.'

The officer retired to the rear of the car. He returned a moment later.

'Sorry to have troubled you, sir; but get in touch with us if you see any suspicious characters about these parts.'

Jeremy nodded and drove on. How awful, he thought, to be a hunted man. To know that it was your wits against the rest of society's and that the odds were overwhelmingly against you. He had previously tended to think of all prison breaks in terms of John Galsworthy's *Escape*, but now another picture came into his mind. It was of a number of recently successful breaks; successful to the extent that in each the prisoner had remained at large for weeks, and in two instances for several months, before being recaptured. A few of them had managed to get across to Ireland; and if you could get there, why not to Tangier or South America? And how much less likely you were to be found in either of those places.

Jeremy's thoughts moved on a stage. The most successful prison-breakers had invariably had outside help. Someone to spirit them away from the immediate vicinity of the prison: someone to hide them, feed them and provide them with a set of clothes. Yates had been at large for getting on for forty-eight hours and no trace of him had been found. Jeremy felt that there was only one inference to be drawn from this. But even so, how could Yates hope to get out of the country taking with him £8,000 in cash? It was fantastic and quite beyond execution—even with help.

Approaching the entrance to the Hall, he slowed down and changed gear. With superfluous care he put out the left indicator and turned into the drive. He was about to accelerate when something attracted his attention. It was a tiny movement inside Sylvia's cottage. So tiny that a moment later he was wondering whether he hadn't imagined it. With interest aroused, he parked the car beneath some trees twenty yards farther on and walked back to the cottage. He peeped cautiously through the front parlour window where the movement had come from, but the curtains were half-drawn and it was impossible to see much. There was certainly no sign of life. Next he tried the front door but it was locked. He was about to walk away, satisfied that his eye had played him a trick, when something else riveted his attention. It was a sound and it seemed to come from below ground level. Holding his breath, he listened till his senses seemed to tingle. The sound, which was very soft, continued. He found it impossible to define, but was more than sure it had no right to be. Stealthily he moved round the side of the cottage to the back door. That was also secured. Here, however, the sounds were clearer and could be distinguished as a form of rhythmic tapping. Moreover they came quite definitely from the cellar.

Whoever was inside had carefully locked himself there in order not to be disturbed. Jeremy stood on the back doorstep pinching his lower lip and trying to make up his mind what to do. The one thing that did not occur to him was to go back down the road to where the police had their control point. With a thoughtful frown he surveyed the small back yard and decided that, if he was going to stay and watch developments, the best place for this would be from behind one of the surrounding stout trees. He reckoned that the mysterious visitor would almost certainly leave by the back door and depart under cover of the wood. The front door would be an unnecessary risk.

Hardly was the thought born before he was across the yard and behind the thick trunk of an elm. No one could possibly leave without his seeing them.

As he waited, however, he became not only less resolute, but less certain of what he would do if and when the moment for action arrived.

After about twenty minutes, he became aware that someone was moving around in the kitchen. A lace curtain covered the lower part of the window and he could only identify a shape—a human shape. A few seconds later, the back door slowly opened. Gripping the tree to steady himself, Jeremy craned his head to get a better view.

The person who emerged round the half-open door, closing it quickly behind him with a soft click, was Hubert Waygood. Without pausing, he scuttled across the yard like a beetle caught in the open and disappeared amongst the trees.

Jeremy waited for several further minutes

before moving. Then satisfied that Waygood was not going to return, he crept up to the door and tried it. It held fast and he realized there must be an inside catch since Waygood had certainly not locked it from the outside.

Cursing softly to himself, he walked back to where he'd left the car.

As he continued his journey up the drive, his mind was occupied with thoughts of what Waygood might have been doing at the cottage.

He was also puzzled to know what had been in the small attaché-case Waygood was carrying when he emerged.

The Hall not only looked, but seemed to be, deserted. There was no one round at the garage which Jeremy first made for and later it was an age before anyone came to answer the front door. Eventually, however, it was opened by Mrs. Drake, the housekeeper.

'Yes, I was expecting you, Mr. Harper', she said as Jeremy started to explain.

'Is anyone at home?' he asked as he carried his suitcase into the hall.

'Sir Geoffrey's not yet in, of course, and Miss Jennie . . . well, actually I haven't seen her since lunchtime. I've no idea where she is.' She moved past him to lead the way upstairs. 'I'll show you to your room.'

Jeremy followed her. He thought she looked worried and from the manner in which she opened his bedroom door and immediately left him, it was obvious that she was disinclined to stop and talk.

While he was unpacking his bag, he switched on the portable radio which had been thoughtfully placed on the bedside table and was just in time to hear the tail-end of the six o'clock news. Following an account of a meeting of scientists on Bogota, the announcer continued in the same neutral tones:

'The search for Derek Yates who the day before yesterday escaped from Franwich prison has been intensified. Special watch is being maintained at railway stations also at sea and airports. The police believe, however, that Yates is still somewhere in the Seahaven area. It was in this town that he lived prior to his recent conviction at the Assizes for stealing eight thousand pounds in cash.' In a deadpan tone, the voice went on, 'The money has not yet been recovered.'

There was a slight pause and Jeremy heard the crackle as a sheet of script was turned over.

'The police believe that Yates may be able to assist them in their inquiries into the death of Miss Sylvia Ainsworth, who...'

With a sudden movement Jeremy switched it off. It seemed that the day had brought no fresh

developments and that the news was the same
as had appeared in the morning papers. One
certainty was that the public were being left in
no doubt that Yates was responsible for Sylvia's
death. Only the law of defamation and possible
contempt of court prevented the Press from
publicly adding up to four the two and the two
which were discreetly separated by a few inches
of newsprint.

For quite a time after he had finished his
unpacking, Jeremy stood in the middle of the
bedroom wondering what to do. The house was
completely silent and for aught he knew Mrs.
Drake and he were its sole occupants . . . and it
almost seemed that she might have been
spirited away after showing him to his room.

He reflected that he hadn't been up to the
main bedroom floor since Jennie and he were
children and had played hide-and-seek there on
wet afternoons. His recent visits had brought
him no farther than the main living-rooms.

Eventually he decided to go downstairs and
make himself at home until someone did
appear.

He had just seated himself on the
drawing-room sofa with a pile of magazines
when the door flew open and Sir Geoffrey came
in.

'Where's Jennie?' he asked, looking quickly
all round the room.

'I don't know, sir. I haven't seen her since I

arrived about half an hour ago.'

Sir Geoffrey strode across to the fireplace and jabbed fiercely at the bell.

Jeremy decided that it was not for him to express doubts on the likelihood of anyone answering it. As well too that he didn't since a manservant in a stiffly-starched white jacket appeared almost immediately.

'Where's Miss Jennie, Proudfoot?' Sir Geoffrey asked in an accusing tone.

'I'm not sure, sir, I . . .'

'When did you last see her, man?'

Proudfoot looked pink and flustered.

'It must have been shortly after lunch, sir', he stammered. 'When I served her coffee in here.'

'You mean you haven't seen her at all since then—not at all during the past five hours?'

'No, I suppose it would be that', said the hapless Proudfoot in an attempted mollifying tone.

With one side of his face screwed up so ferociously as to make Jeremy wonder if his monocle was not going to buckle, Sir Geoffrey glared at the servant. Grinding out each word, he said:

'But I told you to keep an eye on her during the afternoon, didn't I?'

'Yes, sir; but I had every reason to think she went up to her room and remained there.'

'How do you know she didn't and isn't still

there then?'

'Mrs. Drake looked in about half past four to see if she'd like some tea and her room was empty.'

'Get out of my sight before I throw something at you', Sir Geoffrey barked. As the door closed behind the swiftly-departing servant, he added, 'Useless nincompoop.' Turning to Jeremy and ejecting his monocle with a menacing grimace he went on, 'Anything may have happened to her. I gave particular orders that the staff were to keep a discreet eye on her and see that she didn't attempt anything rash.'

'She may just have gone out for a stroll', Jeremy said.

'For five hours?' Sir Geoffrey retorted, as though only an imbecile could have made the remark. 'Anyway the first thing to do is to ascertain whether she's taken anything with her.' He strode across to the door. 'Come along, you'd better come with me', he said as he noticed Jeremy's indecision.

Together they went up to Jennie's room. Jeremy half-expected that they would either find the door locked or see Jennie lying asleep on her bed. But it was neither. The room was empty; and there were no dramatic notes pinned to the dressing-table and no sign of any hurried packing.

'Doesn't necessarily mean a thing', Sir

Geoffrey said when Jeremy pointed this out. 'She'd be quite capable of going off to the Antipodes without either her toothbrush or a spare handkerchief.'

If this was so, Jeremy didn't really see what they could have hoped to glean there at all.

Sir Geoffrey looked at his watch and appeared to do some deep mental calculation. Finally he said:

'I'll give her another forty minutes. If she hasn't showed up by half past seven, I shall phone the Chief Constable.'

'Why are you so certain she's gone off?' Jeremy asked, bewildered by the fresh turn of events.

'I hope to God she hasn't. But lately she's been in such a wilful mood she'd be capable of doing anything—the more spectacular and foolhardy the better. One would have thought that Yates had been proved a worthless blackguard and crook. He has, of course, to anyone with a pinch of sense; but to my daughter, no. She still pretends to believe that he's a martyred innocent.'

'Do you think she's been in touch with him since his escape?'

'I doubt whether she's seen him, though it pleases her to hint at the possibility.'

'But if he's really in these parts, why haven't the police got on to him yet? What with dogs and all the men they've had scouring the landscape, I'd have thought they must have got on to his scent.'

'It could be that he's been and gone by now: collected the money and skipped right out of the district.'

'If that's so, there's surely no likelihood of Jennie having run away with him this afternoon.'

'What's to prevent her having gone to meet him at a pre-arranged rendezvous?' Sir Geoffrey asked.

'Without leaving a note or taking any clothes?'

'A note would merely mean my getting the police on to them earlier; and as to clothes . . . well, she can quite easily buy what she needs.' As a grim afterthought he added, 'they won't be exactly poor with eight thousand pounds in his pocket.'

Jeremy somehow refused to believe that it had all happened as simply as this. Yates had escaped from prison: that was a fact as much as Sylvia Ainsworth's death and the disappearance of the money. But in the short space of forty-eight hours and with the whole of the county on his heels, how could he have committed a murder in the heart of Seahaven, recovered the money and vanished?—all without so much as a smell of him being traced. Single-handed it was an impossible feat.

But a recurring thought again passed through

Jeremy's mind. What about the mysterious and unidentified accomplice without whom the faked robbery could never have been staged and the money been spirited away? He gave a little shiver. He had a headache and felt slightly sick, the way he often did when he was being given a rough ride in court.

The door suddenly pushed open about eighteen inches and through it came Sambo, looking well pleased with himself. His tail flailed the air and he had the absurd body wriggle he assumed when uncertain of his welcome. At the sight of the dog, Jeremy gasped.

'He must have been out with Jennie', he said tensely.

'He has been. Any objections?'

The two men switched their gaze to the door where Jennie was standing and looking at them with a faintly sardonic smile. She was in blue jeans and a check blouse. her hair was slightly windblown and she radiated good health.

'And where have you been?' her father asked in frigid tones.

'Out for a walk with the dogs.'

'I thought I asked you not to go wandering off by yourself.'

'You did. You said it was unsafe.'

'And yet you do.'

'Because it's not.' It was with an air of pent-up excitement that she went on, 'I talked to one of the police officers on my way back. He was over by Piglet Ridge all by himself, looking so bored, the poor pet, I felt quite sorry for him. *He* doesn't think they'll ever find Derek now. He said that one of their dogs picked up his scent yesterday evening over on the other side of the ridge, but lost it after about half a mile and today they've not been able to pick it up again. So it looks as though he's got right away', she added, looking triumphantly from one to the other.

Sir Geoffrey seemed about to say something but then to change his mind. Instead he walked across and pressed the bell.

'We'll have dinner as soon as you're ready', he said as he turned round.

'Oh, there was one other bit of news too, Daddy', Jennie said with a faintly mocking smile as she was going out of the door. 'Your Scotland Yard detective has been recalled to London for an urgent conference.'

★      ★      ★

That night the grounds of Seahaven Hall lay still and mysterious in the eerie half-light of a waning moon. Not far from Sylvia's cottage two men moved through the trees in silent stealth. They reached their objective and for a while stood like mourners round a grave. Then, their mission complete, they melted into the shadows and vanished.


## CHAPTER FIFTEEN

The next morning found Detective-Superintendent Manton returning by train to Seahaven. He was accompanied by Detective-Sergeant Andrew Talper who had assisted him on a number of cases.

The two men were totally unlike and had nothing in common apart from their police training. But it was probably this very dissimilarity in outlook and character that made them a formidable team. Each complemented the other so that little was missed. The quick wits and perception of the town-bred Manton were allied to the painstaking thoroughness of the country-born Talper, and like so many with opposite virtues (their vices have no particular relevance here) each had a considerable liking and respect for the other. In addition, Talper as the junior though the older of the two found in Manton someone to whom he was content to give unstinted loyalty.

For most of the way down, Manton slept and Talper gazed placidly out at the landscape. On arrival at Franwich they found a police car waiting to take them to headquarters, where Manton spent half an hour in private

154

conversation with the Chief Constable. Following this, he and Talper drove down to Seahaven.

They arrived as Sergeant Floyd was returning from lunch and Manton made the introductions as they climbed the stairs to the C.I.D. office.

'Successful trip?' Floyd asked after shaking hands with Talper. 'Didn't expect you back so soon.' Manton's grunted reply was smothered by a yawn and Sergeant Floyd went on, 'I'm afraid there's nothing new to report from this end since you went off yesterday afternoon.'

'No, so I gather. I called in at headquarters on my way down. I think we must now work on the basis that Yates has got right out of the district.'

'Or he could be dead.'

'Dead?' Manton echoed in surprise.

'Yes; killed.'

'Let's have it, Sergeant. What's on your mind?'

Speaking with great earnestness, Floyd said:

'We know that Yates must have had an accomplice—at least one and possibly more—who got away with the money. Now, when he escaped from prison, my guess is that his first move would have been to get in touch with this accomplice. O.K. so far? Right. I believe he may then have discovered he'd been double-crossed.'

'But wait a moment', Manton broke in. 'Are

you suggesting that it wasn't Yates who murdered Sylvia Ainsworth? And if so, who did?'

'I'm sure he did murder her; but I think it's possible—I'm putting it no higher than that, mind you—that he in turn has been killed.'

'By his unknown accomplice?'

Floyd nodded and Manton went on. 'But don't you think Sylvia Ainsworth was the accomplice?'

'Possibly, though it's by no means the only inference to be drawn from the facts. If one accepts the evidence of the prison clothing found at her cottage, it's clear that she and Yates were up to something together, though it doesn't necessarily mean that she assisted him in that particular enterprise.'

'True', Manton said.

A silence ensued and then Talper, joining in the discussion for the first time, said in slow, unemphatic tones:

'It seems to me that on the facts you have a choice of three main conclusions. The first and most obvious is that there was some tie-up between Yates and the deceased which at the moment we don't know of, but which led him to murder her. The next is that although her cottage was his first objective when he got out of prison and that he went there and received a change of clothing, he was nevertheless not her murderer. In that event the button found at the scene of the murder can only have been planted to incriminate him; which of course it readily does seeing that he's the most obvious suspect. The third conclusion is that both the button at the scene and the clothing at the cottage are deliberate plants to show that not only was there some link between him and the deceased, but also that he murdered her, when in fact neither is so.'

'Ye-s', Manton said. 'And you've touched on one point that's been puzzling me from the start. Namely why he ran the risk of running round the Town Hall in his prison clothes.'

Floyd looked at him sharply.

'You mean you think the button *was* a plant and that someone else murdered her?'

'I don't know, but it seems odd, doesn't it?'

'Don't forget it was after dark and that he could easily have been wearing a topcoat of some sort. In fact I'd say he must have been. Also where better to dispose of his prison garb afterwards than in the empty, lonely cottage of his victim?'

'That's a point', Manton conceded. 'And after murdering Sylvia Ainsworth, I gather you suggest he may have run foul of his accomplice—or other accomplice if Sylvia herself was one—and been killed.' He appeared to weight the probabilities for a moment in silence. At length he said, 'Pure supposition and not, I think, at all likely.' Floyd gave a shrug of indifference and Manton continued, 'Let's concentrate on the faked robbery aspect. We've got to dig much deeper into that. If Sylvia Ainsworth wasn't the accomplice—and I agree she may not have been—we must find out who was. Or if she was concerned in it whether there was, as you suggest, a third person involved—someone who still lurks dangerously in the wings.'

'There seems to be one obvious person to tackle on the subject', Talper said quietly.

Manton nodded.

'Mmm, Waygood . . . I wonder just where he fits into this.'

★      ★      ★

'Hello, Mr. Waygood, not gone on your holidays yet?'

The greeting came from one of the Town Hall janitors, who, slipping off to have a quiet smoke away from prying eyes, came face to face with him round a bend in one of the building's darker corridors.

Waygood scowled and muttering something conventional about still being very busy hurried on his way. The janitor looked after him curiously.

'Must be this hot weather', he murmured to himself as he fondly selected a dog-end from the battered tin in which he kept them.

August was indeed producing one of its spells of fine weather, not that such was discernible in the gloomy hinter-regions of the Town Hall where the sun never reached and there always lingered a mysterious and stale smell of kippers.

Arriving at the Clerk of Assize's office, Waygood looked quickly up and down the corridor before letting himself in. Silently he closed the door behind him.

The room had already acquired the melancholy and almost museum-like air that seeped in immediately it was unoccupied for the shortest period.

Walking over to the big cupboard which was stacked with case records, each set neatly tied with a piece of pink tape, he quickly found the one he was looking for and proceeded over to his desk. Settling down, he became engrossed and never heard the faint click as the door opened.

'Ah! The very man we want to see.'

He started and looked up to see Sergeant Floyd standing in the doorway with two other men just behind him.

'Goodness, you made me jump', he said crossly.

The three intruders moved over to his desk and grouped themselves around it. It was Floyd who spoke again.

'You forgot to drop the catch on the door. Careless', he added, shaking his head in mock reproof.

'I don't know what you mean', Waygood said, but would have done better to have ignored the remark.

Floyd came closer and, twisting his head on one side to read the papers which lay open on the desk, went on:

'I see you're also interested in the Yates case. None of the documents missing, I hope?' His tone was unpleasant and this time Waygood didn't reply but contrived to muster an expression of outrage and annoyance. 'By the way', Floyd continued, 'this is Detective-Superintendent Manton of Scotland Yard and this is Detective-Sergeant Talper, also of the Metropolitan Police.'

Waygood looked coldly from one to the other as the introductions were made.

'I'd like to take possession of those papers if you don't mind', Manton said.

'I've got no authority to hand them over to you. You'll have to ask Mr. Swinbank, the Clerk of Assize and . . .'

'I already have', Manton broke in, 'and he has no objection provided I give you a receipt.'

Waygood hesitated a moment and then with the air of a shop assistant wanting to be rid of a disagreeable customer, he started to bundle the papers together.

'Don't leave out exhibit six', Floyd said, picking Yates's original rough sketch up from the desk and handing it to him.

'I wasn't going to, Sergeant', Waygood retorted. With fumbling fingers, he tied the papers and thrust them at Manton. 'There you are. I thought you might be wanting them. That's why I had them out.' Some of his old self-assurance seemed to have returned to him.

'There were one or two other matters we wanted to see you about', Manton said, sticking the file under his arm. Then fixing him with a penetrating stare, he continued, 'Are you quite sure you never saw Miss Ainsworth after you left her cottage on the night of her murder?'

For a moment there was a tense silence during which Waygood twisted a paper clip out of shape and back again. When he looked up, however, there was nothing abashed about his expression or tone.

'Yes, as a matter of fact, I did see her afterwards.'

'I must remind you of your denial of that to Sergeant Floyd', Manton interjected.

'That's all right, Superintendent, I remember what I said to him.'

'Well?'

'I think I'd best start at the beginning and then you'll see.

'As I told Sergeant Floyd, I went to see Miss Ainsworth that evening and found her in a very strange sort of mood. All nervous tension she was; clearly didn't want me inside the house, so

I left in a very short time.' He pushed his chair back from the desk and crossed one leg comfortably over the other. Looking his most important self, he went on, 'However, I didn't return immediately to Seahaven which is what I think I told our friend here I did. Instead I hung about to see if I could discover what was going on. It was crystal clear that it was something fishy and I felt I ought to know what. So I hid behind a tree and waited. After about five minutes or so, I could see movements in the kitchen at the back. There were definitely two people in there.'

'How could you tell?' Floyd asked sharply.

'There was a small chink in the curtains and I could see them moving about. But let me go on with my story. Not only could I see, I also heard . . .' At this point he wagged a bony finger at his audience to emphasize the significance of his words, '. . . heard muffled voices from which I could tell that some sort of argument was going on.'

'How far away were you?' Manton asked.

'Forty to fifty feet. Behind one of those big trees that overhang the yard at the back.'

'Could you see who this other person was?'

'I'm coming to that if you'll give me half a chance. No, I can't actually swear who it was; except that it was definitely a male. But I don't imagine you'll have any more doubt than I that it was Yates. After a short time I decided to creep up to the back door so as to be able to see and hear better. Unfortunately they'd moved out of the kitchen by the time I got there. I then decided that I would have an excellent chance of nabbing Yates if I could take them by surprise. I tried the back door but it was locked. So I banged on it loudly and shouted to Sylvia to open up. It was several moments before she did and then she looked scared out of her wits. She obviously thought it was the police. When she saw it was me, however, she adopted quite a truculent attitude. The point is that Yates was obviously able to slip out the front way while she kept me at the back.'

'Did you tax her with his being there?' asked Manton.

Waygood looked at him in surprise.

'Of course not. It would have been a very silly thing to have done. She'd have been bound to have denied it and I'd have put myself right out on a limb. As it was, she never knew how much I'd seen.'

Manton wasn't sure that he followed this piece of reasoning, but decided not to press the matter. It wasn't always politic to probe a story too strenuously in the presence of its teller. So he merely nodded and Waygood went on:

'The next thing was that she said she must get down to the Town Hall as soon as possible and that I must give her a lift. And that's what I did. I dropped her off at the far side of the square and that really *was* the last I saw of her.'

'Did she explain what she wanted at the Town Hall?'

'No, she wouldn't say; except that she had to check something. I naturally asked her what the urgency was, but I couldn't get another word out of her.'

'Why didn't you tell the police this in the first place?' Manton asked, and added, 'You realize what an awkward position you've put yourself in.'

'*I'm* not in any awkward position', Waygood said. 'Yates is the chap who's in a tough spot—or will be when you catch him.'

Manton looked at him in astonishment and said:

'Don't you see how serious things are for you? Two days ago you signed as being true a statement which contains a number of serious falsehoods.'

'It certainly wasn't so detailed an account as I've now given you', Waygood agreed.

'It wasn't the *truth*', Manton said sternly, raising his voice.

But Waygood seemed impervious to censure. For a moment or two, he gazed calmly out of the window. Then turning to face Manton again, he said airily:

'There were reasons for not telling the whole story immediately. However, you now know it all so let's leave it at that.'

There was a full minute's silence before anyone spoke again.

'Very well, Mr. Waygood', Manton said, 'we will—for the moment.'

Hitching the Yates case papers under his arm, he grimly led the way out of the room. In single file the three officers stalked down the corridor. At the main entrance to the building, he turned and said abruptly:

'I want a list of the names of *every* person who attended the Mayor's party on the night of Sylvia Ainsworth's death. And I want it quick.'

\*     \*     \*

Manton's return to Seahaven coincided with Jeremy's first day as unpaid companion-cum-watchdog to Jennie. Sir Geoffrey had gone off soon after breakfast and before leaving given Jeremy a pat on the shoulder and a final admonitory word.

'Keep her amused and don't let her out of your sight.'

Jeremy had felt inclined to query the necessity for so much precaution but had had second thoughts and remained silent. It did seem to him, however, that Sir Geoffrey was obsessed with the possibility of his daughter's defection. Especially since his previous evening's anxiety had proved quite groundless and each hour that passed made it less likely

165

that Jennie would attempt anything silly.

'Well, what shall we do?' she asked, after her father had departed. 'We've got a whole morning to fill in, then an afternoon and an evening before it's time to go to bed again.'

She had accepted without comment Jeremy's presence in the house and, so far as he could tell, was quite pleased to have him around.

'What would you like to do?' he asked. 'Go for a walk?'

'I've done enough walking these past two days to last me a lifetime. Suggest something else ... No, I know what. Let's go up to the nursery.'

'By all means if you want', Jeremy replied a shade dubiously.

'You don't sound very enthusiastic.'

'What are we going to do there?'

'Recapture our youth, of course', she said with a mischievous twinkle. She seized Jeremy's hand. 'Come on. If you won't amuse me, I shall have to amuse you. Do you remember some of the games we used to play up there when we were children?' She managed to make it sound as though their childhood belonged to another century.

Jeremy grinned. Foremost amongst the games he recalled was the one in which he used to manoeuvre Jennie into giving him surreptitious kisses behind the screening doors of the toy cupboard.

They ran up the stairs hand in hand.

'You were a backward little boy in those days', she said, blithely unaware of his line of thought.

'I wouldn't have thought there was much backward about me', he replied complacently.

'Oh, Jeremy, how can you say that? Why, it used to take every feminine wile I had to get you to kiss me.' She sighed. 'But it was all good practice.'

'Jennie!' he exclaimed in a tone of genuine shock. 'You know quite well it was *I* who did the leading astray.'

She gurgled delightedly.

'Then you ought to feel shame not pride. Fancy boasting about being the first male to give me a shove down the primrose path. However, maybe that's rather an extravagant expression to describe the sticky kisses you used to plant on my cheek. They'd hardly have corrupted Little Bo-Peep.' She flung open the nursery door and led the way in. 'Almost as we left it', she said wistfully.

'Except that someone has shut the toy cupboard doors.'

She turned and faced him, a provocative smile playing round the corners of her mouth.

'Yes, but now there's no danger of Nannie suddenly popping in.'

With this, she flung her arms round his neck and held up her face to be kissed. For a

167

moment Jeremy gazed silently into her eyes.
Despite their sparkling brightness they told him
nothing. Passing his tongue lightly over his lips,
he surrendered himself to her embrace. It was
several seconds, however, before he responded
with true ardour of his own.

After this, the remainder of the morning sped
by, as they happily turned the pages of old
photograph albums and danced to the torturing
notes of the old nursery gramophone.

It wasn't until he went to tidy up before
lunch that Jeremy paused to consider the
change that had come over Jennie. Inevitably
there crept into his mind a tiny gnawing
suggestion that she was up to something: that it
was all part of a well-laid scheme to allay
suspicion and lull him into a false sense of
security. But what could she be up to and why
should it involve throwing her cap at him this
way? He tugged a comb through a tangled
forelock which Jennie had playfully entwined.
No, rather it must be a sign, he decided, that
she had at last emerged from the dark tunnel of
frustration and despair: had finally put Derek
Yates out of her life and come to see Jeremy as
something other than a mere friendly and
familiar prop.

His doubts thus allayed, he went down to
lunch. Just before the end of the meal, he was
called to the telephone. Wondering who it could
be, since no one apart from his mother knew

where he was, he picked up the receiver and said a cautious 'hello' into it. Immediately William's accusing tones came down the line.

'Ah, I've found you, Mr. Harper. I phoned your home and your mother told me to ring this number.'

'But ... but I'm in Spain so far as you're concerned', Jeremy said feebly.

'No, I heard you hadn't gone. Nasty business that.' Jeremy assumed this to be a euphemistic reference to recent events in Seahaven and William went on, 'But it's an ill wind etc., Mr. Harper. I've got a brief for you. You recall my mentioning a burglary case at Franwich Quarter Sessions which Ogden & Salt want you to do.' Messrs. Ogden & Salt were one of the few firms of solicitors who provided Jeremy with a thin but steady trickle of work; most of it criminal and financially unrewarding, but nevertheless work.

'What, the brief arrived already?' Jeremy asked in surprise, knowing this firm's normal habit of delivering their briefs at the very last moment.

'No, no, the client is applying for bail and they want you to appear.'

'Oh, no!' Jeremy wailed. 'Not all the way back to London for three minutes' futile effort.'

'If you'll just let me explain, Mr. Harper, I can set your mind at rest', William said primly. 'The vacation judge is sick and Mr. Justice

Dent is temporarily acting for him. He has said, however, that anyone who wants anything of him must come to his home and that he'll not journey to London.'

'Ah, that's different', Jeremy said, remembering that the judge lived in a charmingly converted farmhouse not too far from Seahaven.

Normally vacation work was shared between two junior judges who split the vacation and sat as occasion required, remaining on duty call the rest of the time.

'How'll you get the papers to me and when is it?' Jeremy asked.

'Tomorrow morning at eleven and there are no papers. Just a back sheet with your name on it. I've told Messrs. Ogden & Salt that you'll call them and take telephonic instructions in the circumstances.'

'Oh', said Jeremy again and this time quite definitely without enthusiasm. 'I suppose the application is being opposed?'

'I understand so; but you never know your luck, Mr. Harper.'

But Jeremy did, and only too well. He knew there wasn't a hope in hell of Mr. Justice Dent granting bail to any burglar after the Magistrates had committed him for trial and refused it. The Lord Chief Justice had recently been outspoken on the subject of bailing those who were obviously guilty and whose liberty would only provide further opportunities for depredation.

Not unaware of what must be passing through Jeremy's mind, William told him the bare minimum and rang off. Jeremy went gloomily back and told Jennie.

'I never knew that sitting in "Chambers" meant literally in the judge's house', she said, when he had explained the position.

'It doesn't. Normally the judge sits in a sort of private room at the Law Courts; sometimes in court itself. But Chambers applications *can* be heard anywhere. Once a judge was tackled on a golf course and granted counsel the injunction he sought in between trying to hack his ball out of a bunker.'

'How very inconvenient for everyone concerned.'

'It has to be a matter of real urgency to hound him that far, of course.'

'How do you mean?'

'Well, getting an injunction to prevent someone taking a child out of the jurisdiction of the court, for example. You know the sort of thing: one's always reading of it in the papers. Parents divorced. Mother has custody of little Gloria when father suddenly scoops up the brat and heads for the nearest airport.'

'I see', Jennie said and added hopefully, 'maybe you'll find your judge tomorrow milking a cow or up to his shins in midden.'

'I doubt it. He'll be expecting us. But it's a beastly bore all the same.'

Soon afterwards, Jeremy was the passive participant in a long telephone conversation with one of Messrs. Ogden & Salt's chief clerks. This not merely helped to confirm the hopelessness of his task but also the remarkable *naïveté* of the clerk concerned.

The rest of the day passed off uneventfully with Jennie maintaining her apparently carefree mood.

Sir Geoffrey returned for dinner but disappeared into his study almost as soon as the meal was over. Jennie then yawned twice in quick succession and saying she was tired departed to her bedroom, blowing Jeremy a goodnight kiss as she went out of the door.

Left alone, Jeremy's mind turned to Derek Yates. It was now over seventy-two hours since he'd escaped from prison and vanished.

Jeremy reflected that he would have given much to be a clairvoyant.

★   ★   ★

Hubert Waygood hid his bicycle behind the hedge which ran beside the road and looked at his watch. It was a few minutes before half past ten. He gazed up at the sky where large, threatening clouds obscured the moon. After a moment's irresolute pause, he slipped away between the trees. When he reached Sylvia's cottage, he walked straight up to the front door and let himself in with the key he had ready in his hand.

Inside he moved with the confident ease of one who couldn't be surprised by obtruding corners of furniture. He opened the door at the top of the cellar stairs and switched on the light. As he descended, he hummed aloud, not from any sense of well-being but for company. It is always eerie going down at night into the cellar of a deserted house and when it happens to be that of an isolated cottage ... well a hum can be a comforting thing.

He reached the bottom of the stairs and looked around for the pickaxe he had left there. It had gone. Puzzled, he started to walk across to the far corner where the light from the single naked bulb fought a losing battle with the shadows. Suddenly a slight movement ahead halted him in his tracks and he felt a cold trickle of sweat course down his spine. He strained his eyes and then slowly a grin spread across his face. It was a sly and foolishly knowing grin.

'Fancy seeing you here', he said, his expression becoming a positive leer. 'I'm sure the police will be ...'

The sentence never got completed as without warning the pickaxe crashed down on his skull.

In the silent, dark hours that followed, what brain he had ever had oozed slowly out on to the cold stone floor where he lay sprawled in death.

# CHAPTER SIXTEEN

Jeremy got up early the next morning.

He had arranged to borrow Jennie's car to get to his appointment with Mr. Justice Dent and was about to go and fetch it from the garage when Jennie herself appeared.

'I think I'll come with you', she said.

'You won't be able to come in while I make the application', he replied in a putting-off tone of voice.

'Then I'll sit in the car and wait.'

'It'll be pretty dull for you.'

'Are you going to fetch the car or shall I?'

It was apparent that her mind was made up on the subject and Jeremy recognized the futility of further demurrer.

'O.K., I will', he said. A few minutes later as with Jennie at the wheel they set off down the drive, he asked, 'How's your father this morning?'

'You're always asking how he is.'

'Am I? I didn't realize it', he said.

'Anyway', she went on, 'I've no idea. I haven't seen him today.'

The rest of the journey passed in silence apart

from an occasional word of direction from
Jeremy. Jennie appeared preoccupied with
thoughts of her own and he for his part was
busy in mental rehearsal of the plea which was
shortly to fall on Mr. Justice Dent's
metaphorically deaf ears.

It took about forty minutes' driving along
winding lanes to reach the judge's house. On
arrival Jeremy instructed her to park round at
the back where, he hoped, she and the car
would go unnoticed.

Feeling much like a new boy on his first day
at school, he approached the front door and
diffidently pressed the bell.

A large-boned female with hair pulled back
into an untidy bun answered it. Her face had a
weather-beaten quality and she radiated
strength through health from every pore. From
accounts, Jeremy surmised this could only be
Lady Dent, who was known to prefer the life of
a farmer's wife to that of an itinerant judge's
social help-mate.

'Come in', she said breezily. Then turning
toward an open door on the left of the hall, she
called out, 'Gordon, here's a young man about
the application.' From her tone she might as
well have been announcing the arrival of the
plumber or gas-fitter.

Almost at once Mr. Justice Dent appeared in
the doorway, looking less like one of Her
Majesty's Justices of the High Court than a

genial old gentleman dressed for shabby comfort. As soon as he saw Jeremy, his face lit up.

'Hello, Harper. Didn't know I was going to see you. Come on in. You needn't have put on your glad rags just for this. Hope the others haven't bothered to', he added in quite a worried tone. In his legal *subfusc* Jeremy did present a somewhat incongruous vision in the judge's hall, which was full, if not of farm implements themselves, at least of reminders of their proximity.

The judge led the way into a small study and waved Jeremy into an enormous brown leather armchair.

They didn't have long to wait before the rest of the party arrived. These were the chief clerk from Messrs. Ogden & Salt with whom Jeremy had spoken on the phone the previous day, a fellow barrister who was on the permanent staff of the Director of Public Prosecutions and a peculiarly solid-looking police officer in plain clothes whose every movement threatened to send furniture flying.

When they were all seated, the judge looked at Jeremy.

'Well, Mr. Harper, perhaps you'd like to begin', Jeremy started to heave himself out of the chair and the judge added quickly, 'no, don't get up—not that you look as though you can anyway.'

Sinking back again Jeremy had barely got out a preliminary 'may it please your Lordship' when an extremely pregnant spaniel clambered into his lap and settled herself comfortably.

'You don't mind dogs, I hope?' His Lordship said amiably. ''Fraid you've got her chair. I'd say push her off except that we're hoping to sell her puppies for a good price and don't want any accidents. Trouble is she has rather a penchant for last-minute miscarriages. Yes, well now, Mr. Harper, I understand you're applying for bail for, let me see, a man named Patrick Goodbody who was committed for trial by the Franwich Magistrates last week on four—or was it five?—charges of burglary. If my memory serves me correctly, he has admitted the offences in a statement taken under caution which was exhibited to the depositions. Er . . . that is I think, er . . . common ground is it not?' He looked all round: at the Director's representative sitting with an earnest expression on a hard, upright chair: at Messrs. Ogden & Salt's chief clerk perched on a radiator and at the police officer trying to look at ease on a piano stool. They all nodded gravely. Picking up a piece of paper, the judge continued, 'This is your client's affidavit in support of the application, eh, Mr. Harper? Let's see what he says.'

Before they could do this, however, the door opened and Lady Dent's head appeared round it.

'Sorry to interrupt, but did you pick any rhubarb? You...'

'Forgot', the judge said laconically, shaking his head.

'Tch', commented her ladyship and disappeared.

Turning again to the affidavit Mr. Justice Dent started to read it aloud, or more exactly he gabbled through it so that about one word in twelve was recognizable. The others followed as best they could on copies which Messrs. Ogden & Salt's chief clerk had thoughtfully handed round.

After a few opening biographical notes on Mr. Goodbody, the document moved on to explain how at the relevant times he was far away from the scenes of the crimes with which he was charged. This led to the further explanation that the police had, throughout their common dealings, both misled and misunderstood him. On reaching the final paragraph the judge slowed his pace down and read out in crystal-clear tones:

'I therefore verily believe that I am innocent of the said charges and that I have a complete answer thereto. I accordingly submit that I should be admitted to bail to enable me properly to prepare my defence.'

There was a moment's thoughtful silence and then Mr. Justice Dent observed to the room at large, 'Remarkable. Quite remarkable.'

Jeremy looked coldly at Messrs. O. & S.'s chief clerk who had drafted this prize document in the apparent belief that everyone was as gullible as they looked.

'Well, now, Mr. Harper, what are your grounds for applying for bail in this case?' The question proved to be rhetorical as the judge immediately went on, 'That your client is innocent? That he'll turn up to stand his trial? That he won't interfere with witnesses? And that, as I have no doubt is the case though it's not mentioned in this moving document, he has a pregnant wife and a string of small children?' He gazed at Jeremy with an amused twinkle. 'Any other grounds apart from the standard ones I've just enumerated?'

Jeremy shook his head glumly and carefully avoided looking in the direction of Messrs. O. & S.'s chief clerk who was semaphoring at him from the radiator.

Facing the Director's representative, the judge continued, 'And you, Mr. Egbert, oppose this application, I take it?' Mr. Egbert nodded and started to open his mouth but the judge swept on, 'On the grounds, of course, of the seriousness of the crimes; their probable repetition if Mr. Goodbody is allowed his liberty; the possible interference with witnesses

179

and . . . ?'

'His previous convictions for similar offences', Mr. Egbert blurted out.

'Precisely.' Shaking his head sorrowfully, Mr. Justice Dent turned again to Jeremy. 'You know, Mr. Harper, I don't think this is a case in which I can possibly interfere with the magistrates' refusal to grant bail. However, I'm sure I'm much obliged to you all for attending. The application is refused.' He got up. 'Here, Susie, get off Mr. Harper's lap and he'll let you have the chair to yourself.'

By the time Jeremy had been released and had collected his belongings, the others had left the room.

'They don't seem to be getting anywhere catching that fellow Yates, do they?' the judge observed conversationally as they moved to the door. 'I suppose there's no doubt it was he who murdered that girl. Bit of a mystery, the whole affair.'

'It is indeed, Judge.'

'Know what I think? You remember that rough sketch he suddenly produced when giving evidence? I believe that was meant to indicate to someone where he'd hidden the money.'

'That's an ingenious theory, Judge', Jeremy said, prudently refraining from pointing out that it was entirely different from the one His Lordship had put forward on the evening of the mayoral reception.

Mr. Justice Dent raised a quizzical eyebrow and with a short laugh added:

'I don't expect I'm the first to have thought of it. Anyway, I mentioned it at the time to the High Sheriff.'

★    ★    ★

Having shaken off Messrs. O. & S.'s chief clerk outside the front door, Jeremy dived round to the back of the house where the car had been parked. He found it empty and Jennie nowhere in sight. After flinging his brief-case on to the seat, he stood uncertainly by the driver's door wondering what to do. He couldn't very well summon her by imperious toots on the horn. Equally he shrank from the idea of poking around His Lordship's farm looking for her. It seemed therefore he could only sit in the car and wait.

One of Jeremy's torments was that of being constantly embarrassed by what he regarded as awkward situations. More often than not they were largely imagined on his part, but their effect was to turn him pink about the ears and brusque in manner.

It was while this process was under way that he heard voices approaching from the far side of a high privet hedge. A moment later, Lady Dent and Jennie came into view and walked towards him.

'Fancy leaving Miss Rawlins parked in the back-yard', Lady Dent called out loudly as they came nearer. 'Why on earth didn't you tell me she'd come over with you?'

Jeremy blushed at the booming accusation.

'I'm terribly sorry, Lady Dent', he stammered. 'I didn't ... well ... it was a bit...'

'I know, I know. Women accompany their menfolk only on sufferance on these occasions. I remember Gordon was just as bad when we were first engaged. He was always trying to put me off coming anywhere near the courts where he was appearing. And when I just came anyway, he'd more than likely ignore me—never showing so much as a glimmer of recognition as I sat there resplendent in a new hat bought specially for the occasion.'

Jeremy smiled nervously. Laughing, Jennie turned to Lady Dent and held out her hand.

'I'll remember what you said about the puppies.'

'Yes, give me a call in about a fortnight's time: Susie should have delivered by then. It's been very nice meeting you. Good-bye.' She waved a hand at Jeremy. 'And next time don't be ashamed of your charming chauffeuse. Bring her in.'

'What was all that about puppies?' Jeremy asked, as Jennie manoeuvred the car out into the road.

'I thought I might buy one, that's all. I caught a glimpse of the mother and she seemed a particularly nice dog.'

'She weighs a ton.'

'So would you if you were in her condition.'

This observation seemed to put a damper on further conversation and the return journey to Seahaven Hall was accomplished in silence.

As the car turned into the drive, Jeremy stared at Sylvia's now deserted-looking cottage. Noticing the line of his gaze, Jennie gave a little shudder and accelerated.

'I get the creeps every time I go past it now', she said. 'I wish I could wake up one morning and find it wasn't there any more.'

She shot him a sidelong glance, but his mind was clearly elsewhere and he made no reply.

It was in a strangely subdued mood that they regained the house. It could almost have been that the cottage had somehow managed to communicate its gruesome secret to them.

# CHAPTER SEVENTEEN

Hubert Waygood's body might have remained indefinitely unfound but for the fact that the police suddenly decided they wished to interview him again. The discovery then that he had disappeared led to a search of all his known haunts which in due course included the cottage; though this was made more in the hope of unearthing a clue to his whereabouts than in any expectation of finding him.

Manton, Talper and Floyd were in the latter's office when the news came through and left immediately for the scene. They rode in silence, each occupied with his own train of thought.

Floyd ran the car up on to the verge just past the cottage and the three of them piled out. Detective-Constable Ingram who had discovered the body met them at the front door.

'He's down in the cellar', he said. As they stepped into the tiny hall, he went on, 'And to be quite honest, I very nearly never looked down there at all. I mean I wasn't looking for his body . . .' It was clear that Ingram had been somewhat shaken by his find.

'What did make you go down to the cellar?'

'No special reason, Sarge. I just thought I'd better have a look there before leaving.'

'I see. I was wondering, though, whether it'd been something particular that led you down there at the last moment.'

Ingram shook his head. He opened the door to the cellar steps and stood aside to let Manton go down first.

For a time the four men stood in a circle round Waygood's body. Then Manton lifted his gaze and let it wander slowly round the gloomy walls. Next he walked over to where there were signs of the surface of the floor having been disturbed. Indeed, it was obvious that someone had been digging it up.

'Looks like someone thought of trying to bury him down here', Ingram said. Manton pursed his lips and continued to peer about him.

Over against the wall close to the jagged hole was a heavy pickaxe and one look at this was sufficient to show that it had been the weapon of Waygood's execution, as well as the implement of floor uprooting.

The hole itself was about the size of a football, but completely irregular in shape. If the murderer had ever really intended burying Waygood's body beneath the cellar floor, he had certainly given up the idea at an early stage. But to Manton it was inconceivable that the digging had been for that purpose. In the first place it would have been too much like trying to chop down a tree with a pocket knife and in the second there didn't appear to be any possible need to go to such lengths. Anyway, there were far easier ways of disposing of the body if the murderer had considered this necessary.

Bending down Manton dived his hand into the hole and pulled out a piece of paper. It was then he noticed two similar pieces on the floor nearby. Without comment he held them out for

Talper and Floyd to see.

'I know what those are', Floyd said immediately. 'They're wrappers that were round some of the stolen notes. You remember the bank told us that the pound and ten shilling notes were in wrapped bundles.'

Manton nodded and said:

'They're that sort of wrapper all right and the odds are that's where they've come from.'

Talper who had meanwhile pottered over to the far corner of the cellar now called to the other two.

'If those are the wrappers, this looks like being what the money was hidden in.'

As he spoke, he indicated with his toe an oblong metal box, which was tucked behind some old sacks. It was of the type which is used for the packing of small arms ammunition. It lay empty, its black sides bearing scratch marks and traces of dirt, as though it had been buried in the ground.

'Doesn't look very comfy, does he, Sarge?' Ingram said quietly to Floyd as he nimbly stepped over Waygood's body to join the other three officers.

Floyd glanced over his shoulder at the bloodstained and untidy heap that had once been so full of cocksureness. It was not a pleasant sight.

'Pity you can't tell us anything', he murmured, addressing the corpse.

'But I'm not sure that he can't', Manton said, overhearing the remark. Without explaining this cryptic observation, he went on, 'Let's have a final look around and then we'll get up into the fresh air.' He turned to Ingram. 'I think you'd better go and phone Dr. Runce and ask him to come out here as soon as possible. Also call up headquarters and tell Inspector Adams the position: say we shall need a photographer and fingerprint officer to go over the place.' He turned back to Talper and Floyd, 'That tin and the pickaxe may both yield prints.' He gave a quick, final glance round the cellar. 'O.K., let's go up.'

A few minutes later, Ingram was on his way back into Seahaven, leaving his superiors ensconced in Sylvia's front parlour.

'Well?' Manton asked, looking from Talper to Floyd. 'What do you make of this?' It was Sergeant Floyd who immediately replied.

'It seems to me that you must have been wrong, Mr. Manton, when you suggested that Yates had cleared out of the district and that I was equally wide of the mark when I said he might be dead.'

'You've no doubt then it's Yates who has murdered Waygood?'

'None now. What's more, I think one further piece of the puzzle has fallen into place with our discovery of Waygood's body.' Leaning forward over the table he went on, 'I think it's now absolutely clear that Waygood was Yates's accomplice.'

'What about Sylvia Ainsworth?'

'Could be she was as well.'

'In which case, you presumably think Yates has made off with the loot after ridding himself of both his accomplices.'

'That's the inference I draw.'

Manton looked thoughtfully non-committal for a moment or two and then said slowly:

'Suppose it wasn't Yates who murdered Waygood. Who then do you think it might have been?'

'If it wasn't Yates ...' Floyd echoed in surprise and after a moment's ponder said, 'Well, if it wasn't Yates, it means we're hopelessly off beam. And anyway if it wasn't he, what is he up to? Surely you don't think he's just walked out of the story half-way through?'

'I simply wondered whether you had any alternative theories', Manton replied.

'No. What's more, I don't see any reason for bothering with such.'

Ignoring the bluntness of this comment, Manton continued:

'I had at the back of my mind Sylvia Ainsworth's odd remark about a well-known local person being a dirty crook—or something like that—when Waygood called here the evening she was murdered.'

'We've only got Waygood's word for that and in present circumstances it looks to me more than likely that he made it up. Invented it to make us think the Ainsworth girl was involved in some mystery and that he had no idea what it was.'

'But it does, of course, fit in with Yates's assertion that he was robbed by a gang presided over by a master-mind.'

Floyd gave a scornful snort.

'Even if such a gang and such a master-mind do exist, there isn't the slightest bit of evidence to show that they come from Seahaven.'

Manton shook his head as though to indicate his inability to find a satisfactory answer to this.

'Leaving that for the moment', he said, 'have you any theories on what probably happened in the cellar?'

Floyd made a loud smacking noise with his lips. He said:

'I think that Yates was either surprised by his accomplice, Waygood, when he was digging up the money—or it was the other way round. Either way, it was Yates who got in first with the pickaxe.'

'You think the money has been concealed beneath the cellar floor all these weeks?'

Floyd nodded.

'There's only one thing about that', Talper said, quietly. 'That tin could never have been in that hole. It's too big.'

This remark was received with a respectful silence. Then Manton said:

'Well, it's a point we can soon settle.'

The three officers trooped back to the cellar. Gingerly picking up the tin by one of its end handles where he knew there couldn't be fingerprints, he carried it over to the hole.

'Yep, you're right, Andy', he said a moment later and added, 'it almost fits in but not quite. I must confess I wouldn't have spotted it. To me the hole looked about the right size.'

'What's it all add up to then?' Floyd asked with a touch of impatience. Before either Manton or Talper could reply, he continued, 'Personally I still believe that the money was hidden somewhere down here, even if the tin couldn't have been buried in that hole. And certainly nothing shakes my belief that it was Yates who killed Waygood.'

They returned upstairs in silence. As they reached the top, Manton said:

'It's puzzling . . . most puzzling.'

Further comment, however, was forestalled by heavy knocking on the front door.

'Better see who's there', he said to Sergeant Talper.

The door was opened to reveal the imposing figure of Sir Geoffrey standing on the step with Jeremy behind him.

'What the devil's going on here?' the High Sheriff asked. His monocled right eye had a feudal gleam in it that matched his tone.

'There's been a murder, sir', Manton replied.

'I know there has . . .'

'Another one, I mean.'

'Who? Where? What are you talking about?'

'We've just found Mr. Waygood's body in the cellar here.'

'I've never heard of Waygood. Who is he?'

'He was the Clerk of Indictments on the Coastal Circuit.'

'That sandy-haired, ferret-faced little man?' Manton nodded. 'You say you've just found his body in the cellar?' Sir Geoffrey went on after he had digested the news. Again Manton nodded. For a moment no one moved and then Sir Geoffrey suddenly swung round on Jeremy. 'Now perhaps you realize that my fears were not so unfounded after all. I told you Yates wouldn't be far away. Two murders and an eight thousand pound haul. Good going for a beginner.'

Manton, who had been closely following every word, noticed a small twitching at the angle of Sir Geoffrey's jaw. It looked like a storm signal and indeed his last observation had been made in such a venomous tone as to rob the words of any flippancy. Turning back to Manton and with icy calm, he said:

'And what is your next move?'

'Find the murderer of Miss Ainsworth and Waygood.'

'That sounds all very fine but it begs the question, and with the progress you appear to be making at the moment, I'm not very reassured. It'd be a good thing if you made a really thorough search for Yates.'

'The net is spread . . .'

'Not over my estate, it isn't.'

'What reason have you for thinking he may still be around this area, sir?'

'Because of this latest murder and because bees can't keep away from honeypots. And my daughter is the honeypot.' He looked at the three officers. 'Floyd knows I've got a point there. Floyd also knows my property well enough to realize there are a good many hiding places he might be using.'

Manton thoughtfully chewed the end of a matchstick. Suddenly he said:

'You could be right, sir.'

'Well, organize a proper search for him quickly before there are any more murders', Sir Geoffrey said tersely and added, 'I don't mind telling you that I'm sleeping in future with a loaded revolver under my pillow.'

He turned to go and Jeremy was about to follow when Manton spoke.

'I'd like a word with you, Mr. Harper, if you can spare a moment.'

Jeremy halted, looked at Manton and slowly came back to the door.

'Yes, Superintendent?'

There was a pause, then speaking slowly Manton asked:

'Who was it you phoned from the railway station on the day of the Yates robbery?'

'Phoned? I don't remember phoning anyone. I mean, it's such ages ago . . .'

'Yes it is', Manton agreed, apparently ignoring the slight consternation his question had caused. 'I just wondered if you might remember. You see, we know you did use one of the public phones there. A young porter named Sam noticed you leaving the call box. But if you don't recall it, we'll try and find out some other way.'

Jeremy stared at Manton as though mesmerized by his words. Then with an effort at casualness, he said:

'Well, if I did use the phone as you say, it must have been a call to my mother. There's certainly no one else it would have been.'

'No, it wasn't your mother, Mr. Harper. We've checked that.'

When Dr. Runce arrived the three officers returned once more to the cellar.

'How long has be been lying here?' the Doctor asked as they filed down the stone steps.

'He disappeared from his lodgings sometime after supper the evening before last', Manton replied.

'Mmm, therefore if he was killed that night, he's been dead about forty hours.'

'Does that seem likely to you?'

Dr. Runce's nose twitched as he bent over the corpse.

'Can't really say till I've made a full examination, but I should guess it might be around that mark. He can't have been dead much under that. Have you finished with him?'

For reply there were hurried footsteps on the stairs and Detective-Sergeant Blane, the official photographer from headquarters, arrived breathless at the bottom.

'Am I holding everyone up?' he asked breezily and continued, 'O.K., stand back and we'll get a few shots.' His experienced eye quickly took in the scene. 'Mr. Adams is on his way over, sir', he added to Manton as he knelt down to take a close-up of Waygood's head. A few minutes later when he was satisfied that he had taken all the photos that were necessary, he said, 'Right, I've finished.'

'He's all yours now, Doctor', Manton said.

Dr. Runce bent down over the body again while the officers watched him. His secretary stood notebook in hand and pencil at the ready, apparently no more concerned than if she'd been attending a meeting of the Women's Institute. She even looked vaguely blissful and, if the truth be known, her mind was dwelling miles away on the new autumn coat she was proposing to buy. The doctor straightened up.

'It looks as though he was attacked from the

front and received a clout from a blunt part of that pick axe—probably there.' He indicated where the helve and head joined. 'The blow must have felled him and as he lay on the ground he was struck with the pointed end. There are at least a couple of injuries consistent with that—deep ones right through to the brain. In fact', he concluded, addressing himself straight at Manton, 'a thoroughly savage and brutal murder.'

'And not, I take it, the sort of attack which would have been likely to have involved the murderer in any injury?'

A tall and rather melancholy-looking officer who had arrived just after Sergeant Blane now spoke for the first time.

'Not the sign of an identifiable print on the handle of that pickaxe', he announced at large. 'It's a poor surface anyway, but whoever wielded it either wiped it clean afterwards or must have been wearing gloves.'

'Presumably the former', Floyd remarked. 'No earthly reason why he should have been wearing gloves for digging up the floor. Don't you agree?' he added, looking towards Manton.

'Yes. Assuming that the victim *surprised* the murderer or vice versa, I can't see why either should have been wearing gloves.'

Moving across to where there was greater light, Manton took a sheet of paper out of his inside jacket pocket and unfolded it. It was the list of names of those who had attended the mayoral reception on the evening of Sylvia's death. It contained about a hundred and twenty names and there were small pencilled ticks against a number of them.

'Learnt anything from that list?' Floyd asked, coming over to where Manton was standing. Manton sounded thoughtful when he replied.

'We've been assuming all the time that Sylvia Ainsworth rushed off to the Town Hall to check something or other in the Clerk of Assize's office.'

'Well?'

'Just this. What on earth could there have been in the office that required such an urgent trip that night?' Floyd said nothing and after a moment Manton went on, 'Since we've not been able to discover any reason for her visit there, I'm wondering whether in fact there ever was one.'

'But there must have been', broke in Talper, walking over and joining them. 'Surely you don't think she went there on a mere whim? Particularly not, if we believe Waygood's account of how she appeared when he called at the cottage that evening. She most certainly gave him the impression she was going to the Town Hall for some urgent reason.'

'The Town Hall, yes', Manton said. He observed the two blank expressions which met this remark. 'For all we really know, mayn't it have been someone at the mayor's party she wanted to see? Mayn't that have been the real reason for her visit? Oh, I know her body was found in the Assize office and that of course is why we've always assumed that the secret of her visit lay there.'

'It's also what she told Waygood', Talper said. 'Namely that she had to check something in the office.'

'Just the sort of excuse she might have given to someone as nosey as him', Sergeant Floyd said, beginning to see Manton's point. 'If she'd said she was going to see someone at the reception, he'd have plagued her with questions to try and find out who it was.'

'Precisely', Manton said, nodding. 'Hence my interest in this list.'

Floyd and Talper on either side of him now looked at it with fresh eyes.

'I see you've ticked some of the names', Floyd remarked.

'Yes, three of them', Manton replied. 'Young Harper's, Sir Geoffrey Rawlins' and his daughter's. At least two of those know a good deal more about what's happened than they've told us.'

# CHAPTER EIGHTEEN

By the time that Waygood's mortal remains had been removed by ambulance to the nearest mortuary and the police had completed their examination of the cellar, it was around five o'clock.

As Floyd locked the front door behind them, Manton, who for some while had been looking like a dog on the prowl, suddenly said:

'Since there's obviously not been any forcible entry of the premises, I presume that both Waygood and his murderer were armed with keys.'

'Not necessarily', Floyd replied. 'Which ever was first to arrive must have had one, but he may then have left the door unlocked.' As an afterthought he added, 'It's not likely that both had keys to a house which wasn't theirs.'

'What do we know about the disposition of keys?'

'This one I've got came from Miss Ainsworth's handbag. I don't know of the existence of any others.'

They drove back into Seahaven and had hardly arrived in Floyd's office before Detective-Constable Ingram, who had accompanied the body to the mortuary, strolled in carrying a cardboard box beneath his arm.

'Waygood's property, Sarge', he said laconically, depositing it on the table.

Manton removed the lid and turned the box upside down. There fell out a wallet which had an elastic band around it and a cigarette case with an enamelled picture of Buckingham Palace on one side and 'With the compliments of the makers of Regal Cigarettes' on the other. There was also a small amount of loose change, a bunch of keys and one separate, not on the ring with the others. Floyd picked this up and compared it with the one he'd taken from Sylvia's handbag. Holding them out in the palm of his hand for Manton to see he said:

'They're identical. That at any rate explains how one of them got in.'

But Manton no longer appeared to be very interested in keys and soon afterwards drove off to police headquarters at Franwich, leaving Sergeants Talper and Floyd to get on with routine aspects of the inquiry, puzzled by the abruptness of his departure.

★    ★    ★

Jeremy stood by one of the big drawing-room french windows which opened out on to the terrace. He had a half-finished glass of sherry in his hand and was peering at it with the fixity of a crystal gazer. The truth was that it was too dry for his palate and he found it difficult not to make a face every time he took a sip. Though of the finest quality, like everything from Sir Geoffrey's cellar, Jeremy quite definitely didn't like it. Being momentarily alone, he seized the opportunity of swallowing it in one gulp, allowing himself a tortured grimace and putting down the glass just as Sir Geoffrey returned to the room.

'Jennie not down yet?' he asked.

'No, sir.'

Though it wasn't customary at the Hall to change every night into formal evening attire for dinner, a gong was still sounded half an hour before the meal. This was a signal for those staying in the house to go to their rooms to wash and tidy themselves—or at least to pretend to do so.

On this occasion Jeremy had returned to the drawing-room and been handed his glass of sherry by Sir Geoffrey, who had immediately disappeared to his study to make a phone call.

'I've just been through to the Chief Constable', Sir Geoffrey continued. 'He's personally organized a thorough man-search of the district tomorrow. They're going to start from here at first light.'

Jeremy swallowed hard. Something in his bones told him that events were moving towards a climax.

'And it's going to be a proper search this time', Sir Geoffrey said in a grimly-satisfied tone. 'Not just a couple of men and a dog poking about.'

'Does that mean that the police have grounds for believing Yates is somewhere around here?' Jeremy asked with an air of vague bewilderment.

'What more grounds does anyone want than the discovery of Waygood's body and all the other stuff in the cellar?' He fixed Jeremy with his monocled eye which had the unwavering blankness of that of a fish in an aquarium tank. 'I can take it you'll get up and join us in the search, Jeremy?'

The question was entirely formal and clearly didn't envisage a negative reply.

'I suppose so if I'm really wanted', Jeremy said without enthusiasm.

'Of course they'll want every volunteer they can get. We're after a dangerous man who on his past record doesn't think twice about killing if it'll further his ends. The more people to look for him, the better the chances of cornering the animal.'

'But where do you think he's hiding?' Jeremy asked in a puzzled tone.

Sir Geoffrey was silent a moment. Then he said aggressively:

'I don't know why you adopt this attitude of surprise that he's still in the neighbourhood. Everything points to it and there are dozens of places on my estate where he might be hiding.'

He pinned Jeremy with a further stare and asked, 'Why do you find it so hard to believe? You almost make it sound as though you had some special knowledge.'

'Good lord, no, sir', Jeremy said hastily. 'It's just that ... well, that prison-breakers don't usually waste any time hanging around obvious places.'

'That may be so in general but it overlooks the fact that Yates had at least two cogent reasons for returning here. Firstly to get hold of the cash: secondly my daughter.' With a touch of impatience he went on, 'Anyway, the police are now satisfied of the necessity to renew their search for him. They're rendezvousing here at four-thirty tomorrow morning. In the meantime the Chief Constable has promised to send some men to patrol the grounds tonight.'

Jeremy nodded. Of one thing he was quite certain, however, and that was that wherever Yates might be, he wouldn't attempt to break into the Hall. It appeared that Sir Geoffrey read his thoughts for he said:

'I suppose you think Yates would never dare come near the house. But you can take it from me that, whereas he was a dangerous man before, he's now doubly so.'

Jeremy remained stolidly silent. It always irked him when anyone made provocatively enigmatic observations of this sort and he refused to give them the satisfaction of asking what was meant. Sir Geoffrey, too, appeared to be pondering the wisdom of explaining himself. Finally he said:

'He's now armed. My revolver has disappeared from the drawer where I always kept it. It was there the day before yesterday; but this evening it's gone.'

# CHAPTER NINETEEN

At half past three the next morning Manton's alarm clock obediently roused him. He was in a dreamless sleep and flung out an arm to silence it. Then he quickly scrambled out of bed before he had time to doze off again.

Standing in front of the washstand mirror he combed his hair and surveyed himself with bleary eyes. He hadn't got into bed till two o'clock and as always when he was short of sleep his head felt as though it had been buried in sand. His eyes were sore and his skin tight and sensitive so that shaving became a bloody affair.

While he dressed he gave his mind over to what lay immediately ahead. Like Jeremy he too had a feeling that matters were moving towards a climax; one indeed which might be reached in the next few hours. He had no illusions about the search. If it failed to produce a positive result (if, in fact, he was ordering his troops into what should prove to be the sunken road) things were going to be awkward in more senses than one.

He picked up his hat and raincoat from the chair, took a final look at himself in the mirror and left the room.

Tiptoeing cautiously down the dark stairs, he all but bumped into Sergeant Talper who was waiting silently by the front door.

'The car's outside', Talper whispered.

Quietly the two men let themselves out of the small pub which had been their home since their arrival in Seahaven. Sergeant Floyd was at the wheel of the waiting car and drove off as soon as they'd got in. The streets were quite deserted and he drove as though all the demons in hell were on their tail.

'Not late are we?' Manton asked.

'It'll be light soon', Floyd replied. 'If we can get started before the sun is well up, it'll be a help. That's the hour at which to strike.'

'You speak with the authority of the secret police.'

Floyd snorted.

'I'm not one of those who regard our job as a game of cricket. My motto with criminals is hit 'em below the belt before they can do the same to you.' After a pause he asked, 'Are the High Sheriff and young Harper going to join in the search?'

'Sir Geoffrey himself insisted on that; also that his butler and chauffeur should.'

'And that's been agreed?'

'Yeh ... it saved us having to suggest it to him.'

'But why on earth should we have?' Floyd asked sharply.

'Because we want to have him present if and when Yates is found. His reaction may be illuminating, don't you think?'

A few minutes later, Floyd swung the car into the drive. A shadowy figure suddenly moved out from behind a tree and the bright beam of a torch raked the interior of the car.

'Turn that bloody thing off', Floyd snarled, shielding his eyes and then muttered, 'The idiot. He could easily have had us pile-up into a tree.'

A young constable came up and peered in at them. Recognizing Sergeant Floyd he said:

''Morning, Sergeant. Thought it must be you: everyone else has arrived.'

'You're guarding the drive exit, is that right?' Manton asked.

'Yes, sir. Constable Maxwell is a hundred yards farther up the road and Constable Heaton back the way you've come from.'

This was all in accordance with Manton's plan which was to throw a cordon round the perimeter of Sir Geoffrey's estate and use the rest of the party to sweep inside it and flush

Yates out of his hiding place.

They drove on up to the house. Floyd was about to park beside the Chief Constable's car which stood alone outside the front door when Manton said:

'Better go round to the yard by the garage.'

This now resembled the assembly area for a dawn attack. It was filled with uniformed constables standing in military rank. They whispered together and shuffled their feet to keep the circulation going in the damp, pre-dawn chill. Soon they'd be sweating and cursing that they'd put on so much clothing. Over in one corner stood six men, each with a dog on a lead sitting patiently and waiting for the order to go. For them it would be a treat as well as a test. Near them a chief inspector was talking to a group of sergeants. Manton made his way over to them.

''Morning, Mr. Manton', the Chief Inspector said heartily. 'This is a lark, isn't it? Incidentally, you been in the house yet?'

'No.'

'I was told to tell you to go in as soon as you arrived. The Chief's in there with Sir Geoffrey and Detective-Inspector Adams.'

Knowing that he wasn't late, Manton could only assume that it was nervous tension that had got everyone else there before the appointed hour. As he walked back round the side of the house to the front door, he looked towards the eastern sky where the first faint signs of a new day were manifesting themselves. Not for the first time he decided that dawn was a heavily over-romanticized hour and that the poets who rhapsodized over it as 'rosy-fingered' drew deeply on their imaginations and in all probability had never witnessed one. Manton, on the other hand, felt that he had had more than his fill of them.

A light shining through the half-open drawing-room door told him where to find the rest of the party.

'Ah, come in, Manton', said the Chief Constable. 'Everything set?'

'I think so.'

'I hope everyone understands that firearms are not to be used except on superior orders?'

Sir Geoffrey immediately stiffened and said coldly:

'That won't be much help to one of your men when he's being shot at by this blighter. Yates is a dangerous criminal and I should have expected your orders would be to shoot on sight.'

Manton looked at the Chief Constable who appeared a trifle nonplussed.

'I think you'll ... er ... find that my orders work out all right', he said gruffly. 'Have to be careful you know. There's only one Yates, but over a hundred of us and once bullets started flying indiscriminately we could have some nasty accidents.' As an afterthought, he added, 'Not to mention the fact that Yates would probably get away in the ensuing chaos.'

'I should at least have thought your men could be told to fire once he's shown himself armed ... I know I shouldn't hesitate to use my revolver if I still had it.'

'Yes ... well, er, shall we get started?' the Chief Constable said quickly to avoid further argument. As they were leaving the room, he raised an expressive eyebrow in Manton's direction.

Outside there was a wait while the men deployed to their various positions. The civilian party comprising Sir Geoffrey, Jeremy, Proudfoot the butler and Mason the chauffeur stood incongruously together by the front door. Sir Geoffrey was dressed as for a shoot, having on a stout pair of boots, thick woollen stockings, a pair of plum-coloured knickerbockers, a tweed jacket, and a deer-stalker hat which, like his High Sheriff's outfit, he managed to wear without looking ridiculous. Jeremy had on a pair of old flannels, a polo sweater and a borrowed raincoat. Mason and Proudfoot both appeared suitably dressed for a cross-country ramble.

In the grey half-light that now obtained, Jeremy watched small squads of solid policemen disappear down the drive and into the woods each side of it.

Eventually at a signal from the Chief Constable, they moved off to action stations.

Just before the house became lost to view behind them, Jeremy turned to take a last look at it. As he did so, a movement up at one of the attic windows caught his eye. All he could distinguish at first was a white blur of a face, but a moment later there was a succession of urgent flashes from an electric torch. As suddenly as it had appeared, the fleeting sign of life died again and the window was once more a blank pane of glass.

★　　★　　★

Jeremy's mind surged with hectic thoughts as he strode along behind Sir Geoffrey.

'I'm so sorry, sir', he stammered as without noticing that their group had halted he barged heavily into the High Sheriff's rear. They had reached the point where they were to take up their positions for the start of the search. Sir Geoffrey's small band was to form a first line reserve and Jeremy found himself covering off Manton.

There was a heavy dew and the smell that presages the closing stages of summer, and Jeremy wished fervently that he had on a thicker pair of shoes. His feet were soaking wet, and suede shoes had seldom been less appropriately worn. As they stood waiting, there suddenly came a single short blast on a whistle. It was from way down the drive to their left and was followed by other similar blasts. The Chief Constable turned.

'Those are the signals indicating the men are in position', he said.

Sir Geoffrey nodded impatiently.

'That's the lot', Manton said. 'That last was the sixty. They're all ready.'

'Right, we're off', said the Chief Constable, at the same time blowing three short blasts on a whistle of his own.

The long chain of men moved slowly forward into the first wooded fringe. Some way ahead of them in a wide fan formation moved the police dogs and their handlers. They were like the scout section of an infantry platoon.

If Yates was hiding anywhere on Sir Geoffrey's estate, thought Jeremy, it was inconceivable that he could avoid capture. In addition to the party which the Chief Constable was leading, a similar line of searchers had set off the opposite way from the other side of the drive, so that the effect was of two hands of a clock starting at twelve and moving in different directions.

As these two lines swept slowly forward through the trees, those posted round the perimeter of the estate watched and waited. The search was on.

'All that idiotic whistling!' Sir Geoffrey

muttered, closing to Jeremy's side to avoid a particularly tangled patch of undergrowth. 'Can't think why they couldn't have used some other method of signalling. Ridiculous to give him all that warning.'

'Even if he did hear it, he has small chance of getting away this time', Jeremy replied.

'I wouldn't be so certain. Ever played that game called "Fox and Geese" on a draughts-board? If you have, you'll know that the lone fox very often succeeds in slipping through the cordon.'

'Anyway', Jeremy went on, 'if we approached too silently we might walk right over him. I should have thought it was quite a good idea to advertise our coming so as to put the wind up him and force him to move.'

Sir Geoffrey looked at him suspiciously but said nothing and a moment later returned to his correct position fifty yards on Jeremy's left.

For the next twenty minutes or so they walked on in silence apart from an occasional oath when someone became entangled with a low, whippy branch or a clutching bramble. When they emerged into open parkland there was a short halt to regain formation and then they moved forward again.

\*        \*        \*

Though the sun had by now risen, it chose (as

did Yates) to remain out of sight, and it was under a grey, threatening sky that Jennie could see an endless line of figures drifting across the distant landscape. She watched them with an anxious frown and bit at her lip. It wouldn't be long now before they reached Piglet Ridge. Without shifting her gaze, she picked up the pair of binoculars from the sill beside her and held them to her eyes. With them it was easy to pick out individuals and she fastened her attention on to her father's movements.

She saw his group reach the bottom of Piglet Ridge and halt. Her father went forward to join the Chief Constable and Jeremy gave a furtive look over his shoulder towards the house. Jennie drew back a pace, even though she felt sure that he could see nothing with his naked eye at that distance. Moreover he would imagine her to be still in bed. It was only a quarter to six now. Nevertheless there was no point in taking unnecessary risks and she could see just as well by standing back a bit from the window. It was lucky she'd had the forethought to come and clean away the cobwebs from it while it was still dark outside. There, Jeremy was looking round again, almost as though he was expecting something to happen . . .

\*　　　\*　　　\*

Jeremy reasoned that if Yates was anywhere, it

would most likely be in one of the caves on Piglet Ridge. That was unless he'd become forewarned by the mysterious signals from the Hall. Satisfied that there was no further transmission of these, Jeremy strolled forward to where Sir Geoffrey, the Chief Constable and a number of other officers were conversing together.

'We'll comb the ridge in closer formation', Manton was saying. 'We're also going to throw an additional cordon round its base so that if he's hiding in one of the caves and makes a dash for it, we'll quickly nab him. He looked round at his audience, who had their eyes fixed intently upon him. He wished, not for the first time since he'd been a police officer, that he was equipped to read minds. 'Sir Geoffrey, Mr. Harper, Sergeant Floyd and you, Sergeant Talper, will be in the group with me that sweeps the ridge.' His gaze went round the circle of faces again as he said, 'I think if we're going to find Yates at all, this is the most likely place . . .'

'Yes, yes, let's get on with it then', Sir Geoffrey interrupted impatiently. 'All this chatter is merely giving him time to escape—or at least to be ready for us.'

There followed a short but awkward pause and then they moved off.

The going was now very different and the scene as they scrambled up the precipitous side of the ridge soon resembled an army in rout rather than an organized search party. Sir Geoffrey himself, the oldest and least fit of all, struggled up with such fierce determination as to make Manton reflect that the flesh was not in this instance out-matched by the spirit. But if he went on there seemed to be every prospect of their having a collapsed High Sheriff on their hands.

A vertical bank immediately ahead caused Manton to veer over to where Sergeant Talper was clambering in grim silence.

'It'll be O.K. once we get to the top', he said with an encouraging smile.

'Think so, sir?' Talper replied sardonically. He halted and, supporting himself by a handy branch like a rush-hour strap-hanger, said, 'Never did fancy myself as a mountain goat. Can't think how they manage with all four legs the same length. And anyway, sir, why should it be any easier going down the other side? It'll simply mean that we fall on our arses instead of our faces. What's more', he went on, obviously delaying as long as he could the moment to start climbing again, 'trying to catch Yates here will be like trying to field a cricket ball in an earthquake.'

'That's why we've left men at the bottom, so that all we need do is drive him off the ridge.'

Manton heaved himself up on to the narrow footpath which zigzagged its way to the top and

Talper followed him. Another seventy yards and they'd be at the crest. Manton felt a tingle of excitement at the prospect of what the other side might bring. When he did reach the top, he found that he was the first there.

When they had all arrived and gathered round, he said:

'Now we come to the tricky business of searching the caves. We'll do them one at a time ...' He completed his instructions and added, 'Everyone clear on what's going to happen?'

There was no reply. Either the climb had quenched Sir Geoffrey's impatience or something else had. As for Jeremy, Manton couldn't help noticing that his attention was persistently wandering.

'O.K., then, we'll go.'

'Over the top and at 'em', Talper murmured to Sergeant Floyd as together they breasted the crest of the ridge. But the other ignored the pleasantry and spurted ahead towards the first cave whose half-hidden entrance could just be seen fifty yards below them.

They were almost down to it when everything seemed to happen with bewildering suddenness.

There was a lightning movement in the mouth of the cave and a figure streaked out and dived round behind a clump of bramble bushes. At the same moment someone shouted, 'Look out, he's armed.' Almost immediately there was a revolver shot and the figure plunged headlong to the ground, rolling over and over with the impetus of his fall.

Manton followed by the others ran, slid and tumbled to the spot. In the brief moment of silence that ensued, they gazed down together upon the crumpled, prostrate form of Derek Yates.

# CHAPTER TWENTY

Yates stirred and, as though they were performing a stylized ballet movement, those around him fell back a pace. He raised himself up first on one elbow and then slowly to his feet. He stared curiously round the circle of men who seemed each to be waiting on the other. No one moved and no one spoke; even the birds seemed to recognize the tension of the moment and ceased their chatter.

'Somebody shot at me', he said at last in a reproachful tone, letting his gaze go from face to face.

'Get his revolver', Sir Geoffrey ordered curtly.

'Me armed?' Abruptly he started to move his hand to his jacket pocket. Before it was half-way, however, he was locked in a bear's hug by Sergeant Floyd who had sprung at him from the rear.

'Quick, search him', Floyd said to Talper who had moved forward at the same moment.

With deft and expert fingers, Sergeant Talper went over him. Then he stood back empty-handed.

'He must have got rid of it', he said, searching the nearby ground with his eyes.

'O.K., Yates, you'd best give no trouble', Manton said stepping forward. He nodded to one of the uniformed constables who had just come up. 'Handcuff him', he added tersely.

Slowly the party wended their way down the ridge, this time keeping to the path. Yates and his escort led the way and the three C.I.D. men, Sir Geoffrey and Jeremy followed behind. At the bottom they were met by the Chief Constable, who was waiting with a group of officers.

The Chief eyed Yates dispassionately.

'Take him up to the Hall and wait there', he said to one of the sergeants with him.

The main party that followed the captive back to the house did so in silence. There was no jubilation, no mutual congratulation and indeed a bystander could have been forgiven for supposing they'd been taking part in some piece of solemn ritual rather than a successful manhunt.

As they walked across the last stretch of park up to the broad terrace, Jeremy scanned the upstairs windows. There was no sign of anyone, but he was sure Jennie must have seen Yates brought in. He felt vaguely ill at ease.

Sir Geoffrey, who was walking a pace or two ahead, wore an expression of quiet triumph. Suddenly he changed course and came across to Manton.

'I trust, Superintendent, that your glum appearance doesn't reflect your feelings', he said. 'It seems to me to be an occasion for relief and congratulation when you capture a homicidal criminal.'

But Manton seemed hardly to hear him. He was puzzled and worried. Something had gone amiss with his plans.

\*     \*     \*

Half an hour later, Manton, Talper and Floyd were back at Seahaven Police Station.

The Chief Constable had declined Sir Geoffrey's invitation to breakfast and had returned straight to his headquarters at Franwich.

Manton was waiting alone in the C.I.D. office when Sergeants Talper and Floyd came up from downstairs. He had given instructions that Yates was to be lodged in one of the Station cells and was not to be interviewed by anyone until he, Manton, was ready to see him. News of the recapture had already got around and he knew that it wouldn't be long before he was besieged by Press reporters who would be wanting to know the answers to a stream of pertinent and for the most part awkward questions.

He was about to speak when the phone rang, and being nearest to it he lifted the receiver. But the next moment he regretted his action.

'Hello, that you, Superintendent Manton? This is Lines of the *Herald Telegraph...*'

'So I can hear'—Manton had immediately recognized the voice—'but how the hell did you get through to me? I left instructions that I had nothing to say to the Press.'

The reporter gave a short laugh to indicate that he regarded this as a very minor obstacle to have overcome.

'Is it true you've found Yates?'

'Yes.'

'Where is he at the moment?'

'Safely under lock and key.'

'Have any new charges been brought against him?'

'No comment.'

'Meaning not yet but that they probably will be?'

'Meaning no comment.'

'I take it he'll be questioned about the two murders?'

'Still no comment and good-bye', Manton said firmly, replacing the receiver.

Almost before he had taken his hand off it, the bell rang again.

'For God's sake go and tell the switchboard that I won't, repeat won't, talk to any pressmen.'

Sergeant Talper departed on Manton's mission. When he returned to the room a few minutes later he said:

'I've told them, sir, and I don't think you'll be bothered again. Actually they were rather hurt: said they hadn't put through any such calls to you. Only one from Inspector Lines of Scotland Yard.'

Manton bowed his head and made a despairing sound.

'Thanks', he said and added, 'shut the door and let's get down to business.'

Something in his tone made both Talper and Floyd cast him quick, wary glances. They sat down and waited for him to begin. He did so by throwing out a question.

'Think we have enough evidence to charge Yates with Waygood's murder?'

'No', Floyd replied while Sergeant Talper was still pondering. 'At any rate not before a few loose ends can be tied up; though I've no doubt we'll manage to do that when we have a cosy chat with Master Yates.'

'Suppose he admits nothing, have we got sufficient then?'

'That'll surely be for the Director of Public

Prosecutions to decide. But even if the lawyers don't consider the evidence is sufficiently strong, there's certainly enough to prosecute him for Sylvia Ainsworth's murder.'

'Ah! I was going to ask you what your views on that were? You think we have enough to charge him with that now?'

'I do', Floyd replied. 'Regardless of whether he admits anything or not. But I imagine you're going to see him before he is actually charged.'

Sidestepping the question, Manton said thoughtfully:

'Of course, so far as the Waygood case is concerned, we have no real evidence against Yates at all. It's just a mass of suspicion and dubious inference.'

'All the more reason to get on with questioning him, so we can convert the inferences into knowledge', Floyd said.

'But if they're all based on a false premise ...' Manton replied hesitantly, leaving the sentence unfinished.

'What false premise?'

'That it's Yates who murdered Waygood.'

'I don't follow you', Floyd said, his expression a combination of suspicion and puzzlement.

'Yates *didn't* kill Waygood', Manton said flatly. 'He couldn't have.'

It was Talper's turn to look bewildered.

'Couldn't have? Why ... why couldn't he

have?'

'Because at the time Waygood was murdered, Yates was safely lodged in a cell at Brixton prison.'

# CHAPTER TWENTY-ONE

One by one the implications of what Manton had just told them filtered through into the minds of his two sergeants. After a time he said:

'I'm afraid I've been guilty of some deception.' He studied their expressions awhile and went on, 'For certain reasons it wasn't possible before to let you into the full secret of what was going on; but the Chief Constable agreed after the search this morning that I should tell you what's been happening.' He paused as though to marshal his thoughts and added, 'Mind you, none of what I say is to go outside these walls. This is for your ears alone and not for general promulgation.'

The two sergeants gave almost imperceptible nods as they leant tensely forward and waited with impatience for Manton to continue.

'The day after we discovered Sylvia Ainsworth's body and were having a nation-wide search for Yates, he walked into Scotland Yard and gave himself up.'

Sergeant Floyd seemed about to burst in with

a comment but when Manton paused, he quickly muttered:

'No, go on.'

'You may remember I hurried back to London that afternoon. That was in order to see him. Briefly his story was this. He admitted that the robbery was a fake and that he'd had the money. He also confirmed that he had handed it to an accomplice before pretending he'd been attacked and calling out for help, et cetera. Later the same day after he'd left the police station he contacted his accomplice who passed him back the money, which he then proceeded to bury in a hiding-place on Sir Geoffrey Rawlins' estate; his idea being to leave it there till everything had blown over. But, of course, that didn't happen and shortly afterwards he found himself arrested and from then on kept in custody. The first place he made for after his escape from prison was this hiding-place—but to find that the money had gone.'

'Seems obvious he was double-crossed by his accomplice, whose name you haven't yet given us', Floyd said.

'He says not: that he naturally accused her—it was Sylvia Ainsworth—but that she stoutly denied it.'

'And you believe that?' Floyd asked, unable to keep a note of incredulity out of his voice.

'According to Yates', Manton went on, 'he

got to know Sylvia through visiting Miss
Rawlins up at the Hall. He used to pass the
cottage going to and fro and one evening
stopped to talk to her. Apparently they fell for
each other and after that used to have
clandestine meetings at every opportunity.
Finally they decided to get married. There was
one snag, however. Money. Yates had no
intention of resigning himself to a small-time
life in provincial England. His head had always
been full of grand plans; the only trouble being
they all required money for their fulfilment.
And if he couldn't come by money honestly, he
was prepared to do so dishonestly. The idea of
the faked robbery was put into his mind by
reading about all the recent cases there'd been
of wages clerks being coshed and robbed. The
only thing was that such a plan required an
accomplice and this part he didn't relish.
However, by exerting every wile he knew he
finally overcame Sylvia Ainsworth's scruples
and persuaded her to assist him.' Manton
paused and added, 'The fact that she did agree
shows the extent to which she must have been
blinded by infatuation. It's all too clear that
Yates is one of those glib-tongued, glossy young
men who can apparently cast dangerous spells
over certain of the opposite sex.'

'And not only over *women*', Floyd murmured
*sotto voce*.

'What?' Manton asked. Floyd shook his head

and Manton fished a file of papers out of his brief-case. 'I don't think I can do better than read you the relevant part of his signed statement.' He turned over a page and let his eye travel quickly down the typewritten lines. 'Yes, here we are. This is the bit where he describes the robbery.

'"... It was arranged that Sylvia should park the car out of sight and be waiting for me just inside the park gate. Provided there was no one about—and there usually wasn't at that hour of the day—she was to follow me into the bushes where I would hand the money over to her. She was to bring with her a pair of wire-cutters to cut the chain which secured the bag to my wrist. Then, by keeping to the bushes, she had a covered retreat all the way back to the car. I was to give her a good ten minutes start before raising the alarm. By that time she would be well out of the town. It was then only a matter of making it look as though I'd been beaten up and crawling out to get help ... That was our plan and it went like smoothest clockwork ... As soon as I escaped from prison, I made for Sylvia's cottage and laid low there. She provided me with fresh clothes and I burnt my prison ones down in the cellar."'

Manton who had been reading the statement at a rattling pace, now took a deep breath and much more slowly went on:

'"When I discovered that the money had

gone from the place I'd hidden it, I was staggered. I felt it could only be Sylvia who'd removed it and yet I couldn't believe she'd have done such a thing without telling me. I accused her—I had to—but she strenuously denied it. I was pretty het-up and she was too, except that whereas I kept on shouting at her, she became more and more tense and silent. Suddenly in the middle of all this, Waygood arrived and I had to slip out and hide in the woods. Soon afterwards, she left the cottage in Waygood's company and I never saw her again. I spent that night in one of the caves on Piglet Ridge and hid up most of the next day. When it was dark, I returned to the cottage . . . As soon as I learnt Sylvia had been murdered I made my way to London and gave myself up . . ." And the last line of the statement is this, "I did not murder Sylvia."'

He put it down on the desk and looked across at his audience.

'Following the making of that statement, the Commissioner, Assistant Commissioner and the Chief Constable put their heads together and decided that the news of his surrender should be hushed up. The theory being that if after further inquiries there was found to be sufficient evidence to prove Yates was Sylvia's murderer, well, we had him and could charge him. If on the other hand his statement was true there'd be more chance of unmasking the real villain by letting him think Yates was still the man we were looking for. We had of course to get the Home Secretary's approval to the plan and after that everyone who knew of Yates's surrender was sworn to secrecy.' He made an apologetic face and went on, 'I can tell you it hasn't been easy conducting an inquiry in those sort of circumstances. Many's been the time when I've wanted to tell you everything. As it was I had to try and ride you off certain lines of investigation, which seemed good to you but which I knew to be pointless, without giving the show away.'

'When did you become satisfied that Yates didn't murder Sylvia Ainsworth?' Talper asked.

'*Are* you satisfied?' Floyd broke in before Manton could answer.

'If the same person murdered both her and Waygood, then clearly it couldn't have been Yates.' He paused and added quietly, 'And I believe that both murders *were* committed by the same hand.'

'Nevertheless, there's a fair amount of evidence pointing towards Yates as the girl's killer', Talper said in a troubled tone. 'What is more he had both motive and opportunity. The former being that he thought she'd double-crossed him over the money.' He gave a small, deprecating shrug. 'All I can say is that if Yates wasn't the murderer, someone has gone to considerable pains to frame him.'

'The same someone also did in respect of Waygood's murder, not knowing it was so much wasted effort', Manton observed. 'It's clear the suggestion that the money had just been dug up in the cellar was meant to throw further suspicion on him.'

'There are other explanations', Floyd said.

'But what the hell reason did anyone else have for murdering the Ainsworth girl?' Talper asked, despairingly.

'Or Waygood for that matter?' Manton added.

'Let's leave Waygood out of it for the moment', Floyd broke in. 'You see, I'm not so convinced that the two murders mayn't have been committed by different people.' Slowly emphasizing every word he went on, 'Who else apart from Sylvia Ainsworth can possibly have known where the money was hidden?'

'Ah!' Manton said. 'That's the point. You see Yates says that he never even told *her* where he'd hidden it.'

'Then why should he have accused her of taking it when he found it had disappeared?' Floyd asked in an exasperated voice.

'You remember exhibit six?'

'That rubbishy sketch he produced at his trial showing where he was attacked?'

'That's the one. Except that he says it had nothing at all to do with that but was intended as a clue to where the money was hidden—a

228

specially designed clue for Sylvia since he knew she looked after exhibits and would be certain to cotton on. But she later swore to him she'd never even looked at it.'

'Sounds a bit far-fetched', Floyd remarked. 'Do you believe him?'

'One either has to believe the whole or nothing of his story', Manton replied. 'What he says is that it wasn't till his trial that he faced up to the possibility of being convicted. But after the first day he suddenly realized things were going against him and so he decided to try and let his unfortunate accomplice know where he'd hidden the money and rely on her to do whatever might be necessary while he was inside. Since no one knew of the association between him and Sylvia—and both of them took great care to make sure no one did find out—it meant she couldn't visit him in prison, nor could he write to her. They were both apparently determined that their names shouldn't be able to be linked until they'd skipped out of the country with the money and it was discovered they'd vanished.'

There followed a long silence, at the end of which Floyd asked:

'And where do you propose we go from here?'

# CHAPTER TWENTY-TWO

Manton wished indeed that he had a clear answer to that question: that he could utter a ringing call to action which would be a sure preface to the successful conclusion of the case. Instead of which he had the melancholy knowledge that the morning's events had proved a fiasco. He felt he'd allowed himself to be carried away by the idea of a *coup de théâtre* which had turned out as nothing more than a ridiculous charade. It was mortifying. However, something had to be done, as dark brooding would achieve nothing. Sergeant Talper now broke in on his thoughts.

'Are we to hear the concluding chapter of the story, sir?' he asked.

'Eh?'

'I mean about this morning's bit of exercise?'

'Not one of my prouder efforts, I'm afraid', said Manton, studying a thumbnail and mentally donning the hair shirt of Nessus. He looked up and, giving Talper a rueful smile, went on, 'After the discovery of Waygood's body it was generally assumed by those not in the know that Yates was our man. Though of course I knew he couldn't have done it, it occurred to me that he might be used as bait to catch the real murderer. The more I thought of it, the more certain I became that it was a good idea, if we could persuade the Home Office to play.' Noticing Sergeant Talper's undisguisedly astonished expression, he explained, 'I was positive we could force the murderer to give himself away, however slightly, by the shock tactics of suddenly producing Yates under his nose. After all, Yates's existence constitutes a permanent threat to him.'

'That was why you wanted to have Sir Geoffrey and Harper present when he popped up?' Talper asked. Manton nodded and Talper went on, 'There are three possible explanations, aren't there? Firstly that Yates hasn't told you the truth about the robbery and Sylvia's death. Secondly that the murderer is tougher than you expected. And thirdly that he or she wasn't with us this morning.' He paused and frowned. 'Who was it that shot at Yates? I never saw in the excitement of the moment.'

'I fired; but not at him', Floyd broke in. I aimed over his head; which had the desired effect.'

'Yep, and you'll have to make your own peace with the Chief Constable about that', Manton said. 'You know he said firearms weren't to be used except on orders.'

'I wasn't going to wait for Yates to fire at me—not even for the Chief', Floyd retorted vigorously.

'Was it also you who shouted out that he was

231

armed?' Talper asked.

'No, that was Sir Geoffrey', Manton said. '*He* of course was quite certain—or should I say he pretended to be quite certain—that it was Yates who had stolen his revolver.'

'You mean you think it may never have been stolen at all but that he reported it as such for an ulterior motive?'

'It could be so', Manton said.

Sergeant Talper was beginning to feel more and more bewildered.

'Then you think Sir Geoffrey is the murderer?' he asked.

'There are a few straws blowing that way.'

Talper shook his head morosely. He didn't approve of unorthodoxy in police inquiries and the mock search for Yates had been all of that. He himself didn't believe such methods could ever have been likely to have succeeded. However, it seemed that the plan had commended itself to wiser than he, including the Home Secretary. Despite that, the bait had remained untouched and it was not difficult to understand why Manton was looking so downcast.

Floyd who had been heavily preoccupied with his own thoughts for the past minutes now spoke.

'I've been thinking and I believe I can bait a better trap than yours . . .' He looked intently from one to the other of the two Yard men. 'But

I'd sooner you didn't press me for details at the moment.'


## CHAPTER TWENTY-THREE

Whatever the search had not achieved, it had certainly given an edge to Sir Geoffrey's and Jeremy's appetites.

Immediately after the police had all departed and the Hall had ceased to look like a battle headquarters, they sat down together to an enormous breakfast. There was no sign of Jennie, however, and no reference was made to her absence, though on previous mornings since Jeremy had been staying there she had always been down in good time.

Jeremy covertly watched the High Sheriff butter a piece of toast and take a large bite out of it. He radiated an almost frightening degree of self-assurance and it wasn't difficult to understand, seeing him now, how he had achieved his position in public life. A man's eating habits are frequently a guide to his character and nobody watching Sir Geoffrey tuck into his breakfast could have missed his streak of ruthlessness. Towards the end of the meal he screwed in his monocle and turned his attention to the pile of mail that lay beside his plate. He delicately slit open the envelopes with a long, slim, silver paper-knife. His eye skimmed over their contents before each was placed in one of three different heaps according to subject-matter. Circulars and begging letters formed a fourth heap in the waste-paper basket.

'I shall be in London all day', he suddenly said as he gathered up the empty envelopes and tore them into small pieces. 'You're not in any hurry to go home, are you, Jeremy?'

'Well, no, not really, sir. But I don't want to stay if . . .'

'I wish you to stay', Sir Geoffrey said firmly. 'Now more than ever Jennie needs companionship. I shall try and persuade her to go away for a month or so. Some friends have taken a villa at Portofino, and I know they'd be glad to have her. It doesn't really matter where she goes as long as it's right away. But if I suggest it to her too soon, she'll be as likely as not to dig her toes in and refuse. On the other hand if I leave it a few days, the odds are she'll be more amenable. So if you'd stay on for the time being, Jeremy, I'd be glad.'

'Does she know that Yates has been found?'

'I suspect she saw him being brought back. Hence her present non-appearance.' He stretched out a hand for the marmalade pot. 'I think I'll phone the police before I leave to find out whether they've charged him with the murders yet.'

'I doubt if they will have', Jeremy said. 'In

fact I don't expect they'll do anything until he's been thoroughly grilled and they've got a statement out of him. Even then they probably won't act on their own. It'll obviously be a case for the Director of Public Prosecutions to chew on and he in turn might want to discuss it with the Attorney-General and Home Office. After all it's got endless potential repercussions.'

Sir Geoffrey who had been listening with signs of increasing testiness to Jeremy's forecast of events to come, now broke in vehemently.

'Red tape and nonsense! If that is what's going to happen, the sooner I get up to London the better. I'll get on to Benstead at the Home Office myself'—Sir Julian Benstead was the Parliamentary Under-Secretary of State of that department—'I'm prepared to pull every string I can to ensure that Yates's case is dealt with expeditiously.'

'But the collection of evidence in a double murder is bound to take time', Jeremy said, feeling that some defence of law enforcement methods was required of him.

'They can hang him just as well for one', Sir Geoffrey replied curtly.

Jeremy decided it would be imprudent to cast any doubts on the likelihood of Yates being hanged at all. Instead he said:

'Do you imagine Yates has been around here ever since he escaped?'

'I'm sure of it.' Then with a faint note of

suspicion, Sir Geoffrey asked, 'Why?'

'It's curious that he managed to avoid capture for so long.'

'Nothing curious about it at all. Simply that no one bothered to organize a proper search in the right place until today.'

Jeremy fingered his unshaven chin and frowned. He felt that things were going on which he didn't understand.

Sir Geoffrey pushed back his chair and threw his crumpled napkin on to the table. As he did so the telephone rang and a moment later Proudfoot came in.

'Sergeant Floyd would like to speak to you, sir', he announced.

'I'll take it in the study.' Without a further word, Sir Geoffrey got up and left the dining-room.

Jeremy reached out for *The Times* which still lay folded and unopened. Through force of habit, he turned first to the sports page and next to the list of announcements of forthcoming marriages. He was about half-way through these (a rather fruity crop from their names) when he heard the door click and glanced up to find Jennie looking at him.

She was wearing a pair of maroon-coloured slacks and a white sweater which looked as though it had been knitted on her. Her head was slightly on one side as she surveyed him and he couldn't help noticing that her eyes shone with a soft luminosity. Pushing back his chair, he sprang to his feet.

'Jennie!' he exclaimed in a delighted tone. 'Come and have some breakfast.'

She shook her head in dismissal of the suggestion.

'Where's Daddy?' she asked.

'On the phone. Then he's going up to London.'

'Oh!' She walked across to the window and looked out over the park towards Piglet Ridge. Suddenly she switched round and said almost tonelessly. 'Jeremy, I'm afraid.'

'There's nothing to be afraid of any more . . .' The last two words came out before he realized their tactless import; but to his surprise Jennie didn't flare. 'Were you there when they caught Derek?' she asked softly. He nodded. 'Did you see me trying to signal to him?' He nodded again. 'I thought you must have. I saw you keep on looking back towards the house. I hoped if he was anywhere about, he'd see it and be warned in time.' She noticed Jeremy's surprised expression and added, 'We once had a complete warning system worked out. That was in the days when Daddy objected to Derek coming anywhere near the house.'

The picture of Jennie flashing signals to her fiancé as he hovered uncertainly under distant cover waiting to know whether he could safely approach somehow depressed Jeremy. His

237

mind flew back to that fateful afternoon when he'd arrived at Seahaven Station and tried without success to reach Yates on the telephone. As Jennie's self-appointed (if unrecognized) champion, it had been his intention to tell him then precisely what he thought of him for making her so unhappy. But the swift succession of events had made that a task of supererogation. There had in Jeremy's view been no need to explain all this to the police. Indeed there had been every reason to leave them in the dark. He became aware that Jennie was speaking to him again.

'Did you notice anything about Derek this morning?'

'What sort of thing?' he asked carefully.

'I was looking out of my bedroom window and saw them bring him back here', she said slowly as though groping to understand. 'They shut him in a small saddle room round by the stables till they were ready to leave. It has a hatch at the back and I guessed they probably wouldn't post a guard there so I crept round to it.' She paused and then said in a brittle tone, 'I don't know really why I'm telling you this.'

'Because you're afraid of something', Jeremy prompted.

'Yes; something that's happened, but I don't know what', she said with a shiver and fell silent.

'Did you speak to him?' Jeremy asked.

'He refused to say anything to me. As soon as he saw my face—he'd heard me opening the hatch—his own contorted into such a ... Oh, Jeremy, I don't know how to describe it. It was a horrible expression: a mixture of suspicion, hatred and above all of fear. He knows something, Jeremy ... and I'm afraid.'

It was at this moment that Sir Geoffrey re-entered the room.

'Ah, so you're down, my dear', he remarked as he walked over to Jennie and kissed her parentally on an upturned cheek. Looking at her abstractedly he went on in a tone that made Jeremy's skin prickle, 'Sergeant Floyd is on his way here. He says there has been a very important development in the case and he must have an urgent word with me.'

'I wonder what it is', Jeremy said uneasily.

'Whatever it is, I know I'm getting fed-up with the matter. I told Floyd as much.' He peered at his watch and made an impatient grimace.

A few minutes later Proudfoot came in and announced Floyd's arrival.

'Show him in; show him in', Sir Geoffrey said briskly, and then as the officer appeared in the doorway, added, 'come in, Sergeant, and let's be quick about it.'

Floyd let his gaze travel round the room, resting it momentarily on Jeremy and Jennie.

'I'd like to speak to you alone if I may, sir',

he said, addressing Sir Geoffrey.

'Better come along to my study then.'

The two men left the room and a moment later Jeremy heard the study door close with a quiet click.

★    ★    ★

'I'll come to the point at once, sir', Floyd said, fingering the brim of his brown pork-pie hat and watching Sir Geoffrey closely. 'The position is that Yates has completely denied both murders and has ... has ... well, said enough for us to want to put his story to the test.'

Sir Geoffrey's expression darkened ominously, though no more than Floyd had expected. In a tone which had icicles on it, he said:

'Are you telling me, Sergeant, that you are pleased to believe everything this scoundrel now says to you and that you have come here just to quote me his lies? Because if so, I regard your visit as an impertinence, the greater in view of the false pretext you gave for it.'

Sergeant Floyd neither flinched nor showed any outward sign of discomposure. He went on speaking as soon as Sir Geoffrey had finished.

'I'm afraid I can't tell you the full details. Suffice it to say ...'

But Sir Geoffrey wasn't listening and broke in.

'And in any event how does this concern me?'
'I was coming to that, sir. You see, Yates admits he faked the robbery and stole the money . . .'
'But I suppose you're disinclined to believe that.'
Floyd ignored this remark and went on, '. . . and says he buried it under a bush close to that Judas tree near the lodge.' This time Sir Geoffrey was silent and Floyd noted that interest had replaced indignation. 'He further says that after he escaped from prison, he went to retrieve it but found it had gone. What we'd like to do, sir, with your permission is to bring him to the spot, get him to show us exactly where he hid it and then do some digging to try and confirm or disprove what he's told us.'
'But even if the money isn't there, it doesn't exclude the possibility that he's already removed it himself', Sir Geoffrey said in a thoughtful voice. 'Dammit the fellow's been at large long enough to hide it somewhere else. It seems to me you're allowing yourselves to be taken in by an obvious trick.'
Floyd looked sheepish for a moment; then said:
'Actually, sir, that isn't quite the position. I'm not really supposed to tell you this but . . .' And here he proceeded to give Sir Geoffrey the full Yates story apart from explaining the final episode of the search. When he had finished

there was a pensive silence before Sir Geoffrey said:

'But the search for him this morning?'

'I'm afraid I'm not in a position to explain the reason for that, sir.'

'You mean you *won't?*'

'Correct, sir', Floyd replied unabashed. 'However, may we bring Yates along here this evening to show us the place where he buried the money? It'll be after dark, of course.'

'Yes, all right', Sir Geoffrey said with icy restraint. After a pause he added, 'What this means is . . .'

This time it was Sergeant Floyd who interrupted.

'What it means, sir, is that a murderer is still at large.'

★　　　★　　　★

Manton walked across the office and looked out of the window with disgust. The sky was heavily overcast and a north-east wind had sent the temperature back into the forties, so that summer might never have been heard of.

It was weather, however, that suited his grey, despairing mood. He had had to postpone his summer holiday in order to deal with this case and that had put him right in the doghouse at home.

Marjorie, his wife, had said she might as well

be married to an explorer for all she saw of him and to this Peter, his ten-year-old son, had added the view that explorers did at least bring back exciting trophies from their exploits. Manton had sighed, apologized and made good his escape, leaving his wife to cancel all their arrangements and remake them as best she could.

As he now gloomily cast his mind over this, he wondered not for the first time how much longer he was prepared to remain in the police. Hours were rotten, pay was worse and one's life was not one's own. Clearly police officers were a crazy breed to dedicate themselves for such a meagre return. He cursed at the indefinable spell which held them enslaved. He knew he would never let young Peter enter the Force. He also knew (though no team of wild horses could have dragged it from him in his present disillusioned frame of mind) that he wouldn't swop his job for any other in the world.

The door of the office opened and Sergeant Talper came in.

'Where's Floyd?' he asked.

'Gone up to the Hall.'

'To bait his trap?' Sergeant Talper's tone was faintly sardonic.

'I don't like it, Andy', Manton said vehemently. 'What's more I had no right to let him follow up this idea of his without knowing more about it.'

'You've done his morale good. He's always chafed a bit at having us around: been certain all the time he could get on better without the Yard's help.'

'I dare say, but that's still no reason for me to have abdicated.'

'You've done no such thing', Talper said stoutly. 'As soon as he gets back he'll put us fully in the picture and we'll go ahead from there. Incidentally, I wonder if his plan involves using Yates again.'

Manton groaned.

'I had enough difficulty persuading the powers-that-be to release him for this morning's little flop. Luckily Yates himself was anxious to co-operate—but I don't know whether he will be again. I don't think he much cared for sitting up half a cold night in a cave with a couple of prison warders. Especially in view of what happened—or didn't happen.' He turned away from the window and walked over to one of the desk telephones. 'This might be a good moment to have him up.'

He lifted the receiver and gave the necessary instructions. A few minutes later Yates arrived from the cells below. He looked sullen, weary-eyed and unkempt.

'O.K., you can wait outside the door', Manton said to the escorting officer. 'Have a seat, Yates. Cigarette?' he asked, offering his case. Yates took one and waited impassively for

Manton to give him a light.

'I'm afraid things didn't work out this morning as I'd hoped', Manton said when he had done this.

'Does that mean you've now decided I *am* a murderer?'

'I know you couldn't have killed Waygood', Manton replied and went on agreeably, 'and since I believe both murders were committed by one person, it follows it can't have been you.'

'Thanks.' The word was spoken with bitterness. In the same tone he continued, 'I don't know why you should expect me to be grateful to you; grateful for so many fumbling efforts to clear me of a crime I never committed. The odds are that while we sit here, the real murderer is busily engaged in manufacturing a bit more evidence to incriminate me. I know it won't require much to tilt the scales against me in your eyes.'

Manton ignored the tone—it was no more than to be expected in the circumstances.

'Think hard, Yates', he said. 'Surely you can provide some possible explanation for Sylvia Ainsworth rushing off to the Town Hall immediately after you'd accused her of double-crossing you over the money? Think terribly hard. Didn't she drop any clue to what was in her mind?'

Yates shook his head glumly.

'I didn't even know she intended going out.'

'You see', Manton urged, 'it must have been something you said or did that made her act that way. You say you told her you'd found the money missing and that you suspected her?'

'And she flatly denied it. And if she never knew where it was, how could she have dug it up?'

'But if you're telling the truth, someone found it all right', Manton observed, 'and her sudden visit to the Town Hall must be related to something that passed between you that evening.'

'But who murdered her and why?'

'If I knew that, I wouldn't be sitting here thinking aloud', Manton replied. 'The suddenness of her departure from the cottage implies that it wasn't to keep an appointment. And if that's so, it means that the murderer may have been taken by surprise ... but doing what?' His thoughts trailed on and then, suddenly snapping his fingers, he turned to Talper and said, 'Where's that list of people who attended the Mayor's party that night?'

Sergeant Talper flicked over the pages of a folder and handed it to him.

'Sir Geoffrey, his daughter and Harper all attended', Manton mused.

'Miss Jennifer Rawlins didn't, Talper said. 'She was invited—that's why her name's there—but she never turned up.'

'Why not?'

'I'm afraid I don't know', Talper replied.

Manton turned back to Yates.

'Do you consider your ex-fiancée would be capable of committing a murder?' he asked, fixing him with a pair of blue, quizzical eyes.

'I know her father bloody well would be. He'd exterminate the whole human race if it suited him.'

'But do either of them require eight thousand pounds so badly?' Talper broke in.

'Has Miss Rawlins any money of her own?' Manton asked, suddenly aware that he ought to have found this out before.

'Only what her father allows her.'

'I wonder if we're tackling this case the right way', Manton said thoughtfully. 'Suppose we looked a bit harder for the missing money. What do you think?'

Before Sergeant Talper had time to answer however, the door flew open and Floyd came in. His tone matched the look of triumph on his face as he said:

'The trap is now baited.'

'I hope you can guarantee that the right person will walk into it', Manton said dryly.

'If anyone does, it'll be the murderer.'

'Let's hear it then.' He turned to Yates. 'O.K., Yates, that's all for the moment. Andy, tell the officer outside to take him back to the cells.'

With a sour look all round, Yates snuffed out

his cigarette and strode from the room.

When the door was shut, Sergeant Floyd relaxed into a chair. He said:

'Here's what I've done. I've told Sir Geoffrey about Yates denying the murders and finding the money gone and I've also told him we wanted to get Yates to show us exactly where he alleges he buried it. I hinted that very likely there was nothing to his story, but that we had to check.' He paused and with a smug expression continued, 'I could see I had him interested and thought I made a point of speaking to him privately, I've no doubt he's already passed it all on to his daughter and Harper.'

'Where's the trap?' Manton asked.

'Do you agree that the murderer would be very tempted to revisit the scene ahead of us, provided he knew of our intention?'

'To make quite sure there were no stray clues lying around, you mean?' Floyd nodded, his eyes shining with suppressed excitement. 'Yep, I think he very likely might do that', Manton agreed.

'Well, he can't without giving himself away.' Floyd threw out the words as they might have been a winning string of trumps and added, 'In fact if he enters my trap, there'll be no escape from it . . . and my bet is that he's already found the bait irresistible.'

# CHAPTER TWENTY-FOUR

During the discussion that followed, Sergeant Floyd insisted that Yates's participation was essential to his plan, as without him they couldn't know the exact spot where the money had been buried; only the general area.

'That is, unless you can show us', he had said to Manton.

But Manton had to admit that though he had been there under Yates's guidance, the visit had taken place at one o'clock in the morning (they had driven through the night from London a few hours after Yates's surrender at Scotland Yard) and that in the light of a flash-lamp, one tree had looked to him precisely like another.

Later, when he was obtaining the Chief Constable's consent to Floyd's plan, Manton had artfully pointed out that since it was the brainchild of one of his own officers, he would be supporting home produce (so to speak) and investing in his force's prestige and renown.

'I daresay', the Chief had said brushing aside Manton's carefully chosen words. 'But will it pay off? I'll not have my force made the laughing stock of the land through a lot of melodramatic damp squibs.'

The metaphor though unusual was clear enough, and after further discussion it was agreed that the plan should be given a try but that Yates's participation must be kept strictly *sub rosa*.

This, Manton now realized as he looked out of the window, was not going to be any simpler than it had sounded. The whole area of the Town Hall was strategically posted with reporters who were making certain that none of their possible quarries could escape unnoticed.

'What are we going to do about this army of newshawks?' he said nodding toward the square.

'We can throw them off the scent easily enough', Sergeant Floyd replied airily. 'We'll make them think we're taking Yates back to Franwich Prison and then smuggle him out another way. Luckily the Town Hall has as many exits as a rabbit warren.'

'That may be O.K. for here but I bet there are some more of the beggars hanging around the entrance to the Hall.' This, indeed, was accurate surmise.

'We won't take Yates through the main gate', Floyd said. 'He and his escort can have a nice little cross-country walk and we'll meet them well up the drive and out of sight of the lodge. As for us, it doesn't matter if we are seen arriving. They won't be able to follow us in.'

'Why not?'

'They'll be trespassing on private property if they do.'

'Since when has any thought of trespass deterred a good crime reporter?'

'Don't worry; I'll see that it does', Floyd replied grimly.

By the time that everything was ready and the arrangements had all been double-checked, it was dark and time to start.

As Manton, Floyd and Talper drove out of the town and along the road which led to the Hall, Manton wondered how many more times he would be making that journey. It seemed to him that he had spent the greater part of his life doing it and that, like the donkey who works the treadmill, this was his destiny.

'I'm glad it hasn't rained', Floyd suddenly said and fell silent again. For all the response this out-of-the-blue comment evoked, it might have fallen on deaf ears.

As the car approached the entrance to the Hall, Floyd flashed the headlights on and off several times and, making a racing gear change, spun the wheel sharply over to the left and accelerated between the heavy wrought-iron gate posts that guarded the entrance to Sir Geoffrey's domain. Manton caught a glimpse of a white and frightened face teeter back as its owner tumbled into the ditch behind him.

'Nothing like the old battering-ram technique for scattering nosey-parkers', Floyd remarked.

'All right until you scatter one in small pieces', Manton replied acidly. Floyd gave a short, mirthless laugh.

When they were out of sight of the entrance, Floyd switched the lights off and drove the car up on to the verge. Making as little noise as possible the three men got out.

'Yates and the escort should be waiting by the next bend', Floyd said.

They were and together they all set off through the trees, Yates, manacled to an athletic young constable, leading the way.

Somewhere ahead of them as they moved a nightingale sang its over-rated song and there was also agitated rustling in the undergrowth as small creatures fled for the safety of their burrows.

After going about a hundred yards, they emerged on to one of the grass rides which intersected the wood. Here they turned left and moved in silent file, hugging the line of trees. Fortunately it was a sufficiently light evening to enable them to pick their way without recourse to their flashlamps. Eventually Yates halted and the others closed up on him.

'That's the tree', he said nodding at the silhouette of a bushy-topped one on the far side of the rise which was flanked by larger ones of a different shape. He went on, 'And the middle bush of that clump behind it is the one under which I buried the money'.

Speaking in a conspiratorial whisper, Floyd said to Manton:

'I suggest that you, Sergeant Talper and I go across. We don't want everyone milling around there'. He turned to one of the constables who was part of the escort, 'Here, hand me that shovel', he ordered and turning back to Manton he went on, 'I also suggest that I lead the way.'

Taking huge steps and lifting his feet up high as though to avoid imaginary trip wires, he crossed the wide, grassy strip. Manton followed with Talper who was irrelevantly reminded of a game called 'Grandmother's Footsteps' which he had played at a tender age with his elder sisters.

When they reached the far side, Floyd switched on his flashlamp and directed the beam on to the ground. Two more strides brought him to the tree. In an irregular semi-circle around it were a number of rhododendron bushes and it was one of these that Yates had indicated. Shining his lamp at the base of the bush in question, he let out an 'Ah!' and said exultantly:

'Somebody's been here all right. You can see the earth has been disturbed.' He leant the shovel against the tree. 'No point in our doing any digging.' Then after a pause, he asked, 'Is that where Yates showed you before?'

'It looks to be the same place', Manton said. 'I remember it was one of the middle bushes.' He switched on his own lamp and shone it in turn at each of the other bushes, which, he observed, showed similar signs of disturbance round their roots.

Floyd straightened up. His eyes shone brightly in the reflected light and his voice quivered with excitement when he spoke.

'My trap's been sprung. So now up to the Hall.'

⋆     ⋆     ⋆

'You go on and I'll catch you up', Floyd said abruptly soon after they had moved off.

Immediately he turned back and recrossed the path to where the Judas tree stood with its fringe of satellite bushes. It was the bush which Yates had recently indicated that reclaimed his attention. He played the beam of his torch wide all round its base, eventually bending down and peering carefully at the ground.

When he had finished, he straightened up and at once hurried after the others, moving deftly and quietly through the trees. Satisfied with his final check-up and with the whole evening's course so far, he felt more than ever hopeful that things were going to work out as he had planned them—despite setbacks. Scotland Yard might be the glamour establishment with an international reputation, but its officers weren't the only ones who had brains—even if it did sometimes pay to let them think so.

Much would still depend on what happened

when they arrived at the Hall, but Floyd was now confident he'd be able to hold the initiative. Smiling grimly to himself, he emerged on to the drive. He heard feet crunching ahead of him and quickened his step.

★    ★    ★

At the Hall, dinner was finished and a council of war was being held in the drawing-room. Or to be more exact, Sir Geoffrey was sitting wrapped in glowering concentration; Jennie was staring into outer space and Jeremy fidgeted nervously beside her on the sofa waiting for someone to speak.

Eventually with a heavily resigned air Sir Geoffrey said:

'It seems we can only await events.'

A moment later Jennie remarked:

'I think I heard a car door slam then.' Sir Geoffrey and Jeremy both cocked their heads attentively. 'And there's the front door bell', she added.

'Don't forget what I've said', Sir Geoffrey remarked quickly. 'Leave this to me.'

The door opened and Proudfoot announced: 'The police, sir.'

Standing there in his white jacket with the three officers grouped in the doorway behind him and the occupants of the room gazing expectantly towards them, they presented the sort of tableau that might have appealed to an artist as a modern microcosmic conception of the last judgement. It lasted but a fleeting moment and then Manton came forward followed by the other two officers.

'I'd be glad if we might have a word with yourself and Miss Rawlins and Mr. Harper, sir', he said, addressing Sir Geoffrey.

Before replying, the High Sheriff imperiously waved away Proudfoot, who was still hovering by the door.

'Is this something to do with the ... the experiment you've been conducting, the matter Sergeant Floyd came to see me about this morning?' he asked in a disdainful tone as soon as the door was shut.

'Yes, sir.'

'Have you now satisfied yourself as to whether or not Yates is the murderer?'

'I have, sir ... he is *not*.'

As he spoke, Manton took a pace nearer the sofa and Talper and Floyd did the same. It was a small movement but the atmosphere seemed immediately to become more menacing.

'Then have you come here to make an arrest?' Sir Geoffrey asked bleakly.

'To make further inquiries, sir', Manton corrected.

Sir Geoffrey appeared to ponder this while Jennie and Jeremy kept their eyes glued on him.

'I think I must ask you to postpone these further inquiries until I've had an opportunity to consult my lawyers in London.'

'Surely you'd first like to hear what they are, sir, before deciding on that', Manton said.

'Well?'

'I believe Sergeant Floyd told you this morning about Yates's allegation that he hid the stolen money on your estate and after his escape from prison found it had gone?'

'Yes; and some nonsense about the sketch he drew being a clue to where he'd buried it.'

'That's what he says, sir. The point is there's no money hidden there now. That's quite certain.'

'Are you suggesting, officer, that I've dug it up myself?' Sir Geoffrey's tone was as incredulous as if he'd been accused of stooping to pick a farthing out of a dirty gutter. He went on, 'That I've committed murders in order to conceal my theft of a few paltry pounds ... which anyway were my own, or at any rate my company's?'

'No, sir, I'm not suggesting any of those things', Manton said quietly, flinching slightly under Sir Geoffrey's alarming glare. He found the High Sheriff's trick of shooting up one eyebrow to release his monocle and then freezing his expression most disconcerting. 'What I was going on to say, sir, was that since Sergeant Floyd spoke to you this morning, *someone* has been nosing around where the money is supposed to have been buried.'

'What if they have been?'

'I'd like to ask them why?'

Sir Geoffrey shrugged his shoulders to indicate that he considered he was dealing with an imbecile and shot a quick look at Jennie and Jeremy on the sofa.

'I don't know how you expect us to tell you. However, if you think you know who this person is, ask away; though I can assure you it wasn't myself.'

'I'm not aware of the identity of the person at the moment, but if I might examine the clothing which each of you was wearing during the day, I can probably find out.' Sir Geoffrey's expression became one of patent astonishment but Manton noticed that Jeremy had gone very white. Nobody said anything. 'Are you willing to let me do that?'

His tone was so calculatedly disarming that any refusal must appear deeply suspicious. This much was apparent to Sir Geoffrey, who had the ugly feeling of having been out-jockeyed.

'Speaking for myself, I am', he said perfunctorily. Manton looked across to the sofa and received small nods from Jennie and Jeremy.

'Right, can we go upstairs and make a quick inspection then?' As they filed out of the room, he whispered to Talper and Floyd, 'I'll go with the great man. You, Sergeant Floyd, go with Miss Rawlins and you, Andy, with young Harper.'

At the top of the stairs they paired off to go their different ways.

Manton and Sir Geoffrey were the first to emerge again on to the landing. Shortly afterwards they were joined by Jennie and Sergeant Floyd.

'Nothing on any of her stuff', Floyd said in a quiet aside.

'Nor on his', Manton murmured in reply.

Sir Geoffrey and Jennie had moved together and were standing in silent communion at the top of the stairs. They gave the appearance of being determined not to go down until Jeremy had reappeared in one piece.

When at last his bedroom door did open, he came through it looking like a sleep-walker. Behind him there followed the solid bulk of Sergeant Talper, holding a pair of shoes in his hand. He strode over to Manton and Floyd and turning the shoes soles uppermost, he said:

'See. Also round the bottom of the trouser legs.'

Manton nodded and turned to find Sir Geoffrey had taken up a stance against the banister rail with Jennie and Jeremy making as though to rush downstairs.

'One moment, Mr. Harper', he said crisply. 'These marks on your shoes and trousers seem to indicate that it's you who has been showing interest in the spot where the money was buried.' He paused a moment. 'I'd better explain. After he left here this morning, Sergeant Floyd ringed the area with a paste which we use on these occasions—it has an indelible colour—so that anyone who went there would be bound to get traces of it on his shoes and clothing ... as you have, Mr. Harper. Now perhaps you'd like to do some explaining.'

'Don't say anything, Jeremy', Sir Geoffrey cut in. 'You'd best not speak without legal advice.'

'But Mr. Harper *is* a lawyer', Manton said.

'Yes', Jeremy added, 'and anyway why shouldn't I tell the police the reason I went there? There was nothing wrong in what I did.'

Sir Geoffrey swung round and seemed about to rip him with verbal fury. But when he spoke, his voice was surprisingly calm.

'No, all right. Go ahead then.'

But this appeared more easily suggested than accomplished and Jeremy's uneasiness clearly increased.

'Well, Mr. Harper?' Manton said sternly.

'I er ... er ... I ... I just went to have a look there. I didn't intend any harm.'

Manton gave him a pitying look.

'That's extremely naïve, Mr. Harper. Wouldn't you like to think again?'

260

'It's the truth', Jeremy said with a gulp.

A tense silence fell; broken by Sir Geoffrey who said:

'I hope you're now wiser, officer, as to who is your murderer. I know I'm not.' He moved to the top of the stairs. 'Come on, Jennie, we'll go back to the drawing-room.'

'Wait', Manton called in a quietly compelling tone. Then addressing himself to Jeremy, he said, 'How did you know *where* to look?'

'I don't follow you.'

'You don't have to. Just answer the question.'

'How did I know the money was supposed to have been buried near the Judas tree?' Jeremy asked.

Manton nodded, his eyes sparkling and every nerve suddenly on the alert.

'That's where Sir Geoffrey told me it'd been hidden.'

'And how did you know, sir?'

The question cut through the air like a small and deadly dart.

'Because Sergeant Floyd told me so this morning.'

'That's right', Floyd agreed. 'I told him what you passed on to us: namely that Yates had said he'd buried the cash near the Judas tree on Sir Geoffrey's estate.'

Manton looked at him between narrowed lids.

'No', he said, slowly shaking his head from side to side. 'I never mentioned Judas tree . . . for the simple reason I didn't know its name.'

For a brief moment Sergeant Floyd looked taken aback, then with a shrug he said:

'But that's where Yates told you . . .'

Again Manton shook his head.

'He never mentioned what sort of tree it was. In fact he told me he couldn't remember its correct name.'

'He didn't know a rose from a wallflower', Sir Geoffrey broke in with a snort.

'But he marked it on that sketch he produced at his trial', Floyd protested.

'Have another look at it', Manton said, fishing the exhibit from an inside pocket of his jacket and dangling it for him to see. Floyd's expression as he stared at the sketch became a blank mask.

'It says lilac tree', Jeremy cut in.

'Judas tree, lilac tree, I haven't the slightest idea what you're getting at, officer', Sir Geoffrey said in a petulant tone. 'What's more, I'm beginning to have doubts whether you know yourself.'

'Doesn't anyone notice anything about the words "lilac tree" on this document?' Manton asked, his gaze skimming from one face to another.

With an impatient gesture, Sir Geoffrey turned away but the others craned their heads to look again.

'They're in quote marks', Jeremy observed diffidently.

Manton nodded.

'Precisely. You see Yates says that the first time he saw the Judas tree in bloom, he called it lilac and after that it became one of those little private jokes between Sylvia Ainsworth and himself.'

'You mean that when he put lilac tree, he intended it should be understood as Judas tree?' Jeremy asked.

'By Sylvia, yes', Manton replied. He held up the now somewhat crumpled-looking piece of paper in his hand. 'This sketch is just an ingenious piece of false evidence.'

There was an agonizing pause in which the only movement was Jennie putting out a hand for Jeremy to take gently into his. The steady tick of the grandfather clock in the hall below seemed suddenly to dominate all their worlds.

At length Manton spoke again and it sounded as though his voice was coming from a great distance.

'There's only one person who can have known it was a Judas tree. That's the person who interpreted the sketch aright and dug the money up after Yates had gone off to prison . . . the same person who has now fallen into his own trap.'

# CHAPTER TWENTY-FIVE

Several hours later as Seahaven lay silent and sleeping under the night sky, two men twisted restlessly in their adjoining cells at the police station.

With sudden resolution, Floyd flung himself off the hard bed and tiptoed across to the corner where a heating pipe ran through to the next cell, leaving a narrow inter-communicating crack.

Kneeling down he put his head against the pipe, which ran a foot above floor level.

'Yates, can you hear me?' he hissed. The restless sounds next door suddenly ceased. 'I want to talk to you, Yates.' The silence continued. 'I think we can help each other', he said in a coaxing tone.

Soft sounds of movement came to his ears and he knew he had succeeded in arousing Yates's interest. A moment later, he heard Yates's voice.

'How?'

Floyd adjusted his position so that he could lower his tone and still be heard.

'By your giving certain evidence . . . Can you hear all right?'

'Go on.'

'Listen, I know they've got no real evidence

against me but I want to be doubly sure. If you tell the court that you never hid the money by that bloody Judas tree at all; that it's somewhere beyond reach, it'll cast further doubts on the evidence of what's happened to it. It doesn't matter if you're not believed—which you're unlikely to be. The fact that you're telling yet another story will create doubts fatal to the prosecution's flimsy case against me.' He paused, took a breath, and asked, 'Well?'

'Why *should* I help you?' Yates asked in a suspicious tone. Floyd permitted himself a grim little smile. It seemed that his fish was half-hooked.

'I thought you'd probably ask that, and you'll find I'm ready to make you an attractive offer.' Slowly emphasizing each word, he went on, 'Four thousand pounds is what I had in mind: fifty per cent of the takings ... with interest, which will be quite considerable by the time you get out.'

'Where's the money now?' Yates asked with momentary eagerness.

'Where no one will find it', Floyd said tersely. 'Well, what do you say?'

'How do I know you'll keep your side of the bargain?'

'You just have to take my word for it. It's an extremely generous offer, considering it'll cost you nothing except another small piece of painless perjury.'

A long silence ensued, but Floyd knew that Yates still lingered the other side of the crack.

'Before I give you an answer', Yates said at last, 'I'd like to know one thing for certain. Was it you who murdered Sylvia?'

Floyd silently cursed the fellow. There seemed no end to his questions and this was neither the time nor place for protracted negotiations. Biting back his impatience he said:

'I was sorry that had to be. But I saw her returning to the Town Hall that evening and I could tell from her expression something was up. I guessed she'd come to check on that blasted exhibit of yours and unluckily I still had it. I'd removed it from the office after your trial and Sylvia had caught me in there. She didn't suspect anything then, but after your showdown with her she obviously did start having a few suspicions and as soon as she'd found the sketch *was* missing, I'd have been in the muck.' He paused and as if to round-off his explanation added, 'I didn't act until I was quite certain that was what she'd gone there for.'

And it's all your bloody fault for escaping, he savagely thought to himself. God knows he hadn't wanted to commit murder. If Yates had stopped behind bars, there'd have been no murders and he, Floyd, would have been able to resign quietly from the police and fade away with the money—money which Rawlins Paper Mills could well afford to lose and to which he was as much entitled as Yates. He was sick of being permanently on the unprofitable side of the law: of being a miserably-paid Detective-Sergeant who was expected to spend long, slogging hours outwitting crooks who rolled in ill-gotten wealth. Well, he'd attempted to redress that balance when the opportunity came and what had happened? And all because of Yates's unforeseen escape. Yates's voice now recalled his thoughts from the bitter paths they were traversing.

'So that was why she rushed down to the Town Hall. She'd guessed it might be you and wanted to check on my exhibit. And Waygood? You killed him too?'

'Death's always an occupational hazard with busy-bodies like him. I warned him, too, to lay off his amateur sleuthing; but he was the sort that never learns until too late. He came nosing round the cottage and caught me when I was trying to make it appear that the money had been hidden there all the time.'

There was another silence before Yates said accusingly:

'You not only tried to frame me for both murders but you actually tried to murder me yourself. You did take a deliberate pot-shot at me with your revolver, didn't you?'

Floyd decided there was no point in admitting this nor that he had removed Sir Geoffrey's revolver on one of his visits to the Hall with the express intention of throwing suspicion on Yates and of providing a ready excuse for future search parties to be armed. Instead he said:

'Look, Yates, let's get this straight. I'm not offering you anything out of friendship. I don't like you any more than I expect you to like me. My proposition is a strictly business one, so what about it?'

'Of course I could now tell Manton that you've confessed to both murders.' This time Yates's tone was both sly and vindictive. It was met by a note of exasperation in Floyd's when he answered.

'I wondered whether you'd try that on. If that's the way you feel, go ahead and tell him, but remember that I'll just as quickly deny it all and in addition point out the excellent motives you have for lying about me.' He went on scornfully, 'And if you really believe that the word of a self-confessed perjurer is likely to be accepted before mine, you're a triple idiot. No, my friend, I'd hardly have spoken as I have if I'd thought I was in any danger of being compromised.' Then in final dismissal of the matter, he concluded, 'Think it over if you want to. But remember this. Even though there's nothing I can do to save you spending the next few years in prison, I can and do offer you four thousand pounds plus when you come out. A big return for a negligible service.'

★      ★      ★

Yates did think it over, though he later realized his mind had been made up from the moment when Floyd had callously, almost casually, admitted to Sylvia's murder. Whatever his other defects of character, he didn't add to them by betraying for a handful of silver the memory of the woman he had loved.

And the money? Floyd was at least right about that. It was never found. Manton's final view was that it would probably be unearthed several thousand years hence and cause an excited flutter amongst the archaeologists of that day.

Its mysterious elusiveness, he felt, provided the case with the sort of astringent ending it merited.

This was not, however, a universal view and it was some time before Jeremy's father-in-law ceased to inveigh on the subject—in fact not until he had a grandson to occupy his spare thoughts.

›› If you've enjoyed this book and would like to discover more great vintage crime and thriller titles, as well as the most exciting crime and thriller authors writing today, visit: ››

# The Murder Room
## Where Criminal Minds Meet

**themurderroom.com**

www.ingramcontent.com/pod-product-compliance
Ingram Content Group UK Ltd.
Pitfield, Milton Keynes, MK11 3LW, UK
UKHW040434280225
455666UK00003B/62

9 781471 907685